RAVES FOR JOANNE PENCE

COOK'S NIGHT OUT

"Fans have much to celebrate . . . entertainment."

—*Mystery News*

"Lucille Ball meets *The Streets of San Francisco* in this comedic farce within a first-rate police procedural. This one is definitely a centerpiece of this series!"

—*Tales from a Red Herring*

"Tasty and tempting reading."

—*Romantic Times*

"A feast for the reader's senses. . . . The author has a wicked flair for light humor. . . . A delightful reading concoction."

—*Gothic Journal*

COOKING MOST DEADLY

"Charmingly detailed. . . . Pence's tongue-in-cheek humor keeps us grinning."

—*San Francisco Chronicle*

"Another delightful adventure. . . . Joanne Pence provides laughter, love, and cold chills."

—Carolyn Hart

"This series just keeps getting better and better."

—*Literary Times*

"Action-packed plots touched with an engaging sense of humor are hallmarks of the magnetic Ms. Pence's work."

—*Romantic Times*

COOKING UP TROUBLE

"A tasty treat for all mystery and suspense lovers who like food for thought, murder, and a stab at romance. This is Pence's best mystery yet. So settle yourself on a nice comfortable chair, put your feet up, enjoy a dinner without calories, and a terrific read."

—*Armchair Detective*

"Soybeans have never been so dangerous, or so funny, as in Joanne Pence's *Cooking Up Trouble*. A deliciously wicked read. Don't miss one tasty bite."

—Jacqueline Girder

"Once again Joanne Pence serves up a feast of mystery, humor, and nicely observed human relationships. Sinfully funny writing and plot twists make this a flavorful dish!"

—*Mystery Scene*

"Motives, secret agendas, red herrings, and suspects are prolific in [this] fast-paced plot. Author Joanne Pence has hit her stride in this third installment of her popular romantic mystery series."

—*Gothic Journal*

TOO MANY COOKS

"A tasty little dish of suspense, romance and enough tart humor to please the most discriminating of tastes. Joanne Pence is a master chef."

—*Mystery Scene*

"Joanne Pence again proves that she is a major talent on the rise with her continuing fast-paced, humorous, and sexy suspense stories."

—*Romantic Times*

BOOKS BY JOANNE PENCE

Something's Cooking
Too Many Cooks
Cooking Up Trouble
Cooking Most Deadly
Cook's Night Out
Cooks Overboard

Published by HarperPaperbacks

Cooks Overboard

Joanne Pence

HarperPaperbacks
A Division of HarperCollins Publishers

📖 HarperPaperbacks
A Division of HarperCollins*Publishers*
10 East 53rd Street, New York, NY 10022-5299

This is a work of fiction. The characters, incidents, and
dialogues are products of the author's imagination and are
not to be construed as real. Any resemblance to actual
events or persons, living or dead, is entirely coincidental.

Cover illustration © 1998 by Tom Hallman

First printing: December 1998

Printed in the United States of America

Visit HarperPaperbacks on the World Wide Web at
http://www.harpercollins.com

❖ 10 9 8 7 6 5 4

This book is dedicated to the memory of my father
Robert Joseph "Poncho" Lopez
1921–1997

1

From the pier a massive boom swung boxcar-sized containers onto the ship. First, they filled the freighter's hold, then were stacked three and four high on the main deck. Instead of the officers and crew creating a welcoming, partylike atmosphere for arriving passengers, this crew was busy working.

Angelina Amalfi looked up at the freighter with trepidation. The *Valhalla* wasn't the least bit inviting. Dark gray and white, its main deck was long and flat, and at the back was a huge structure several stories high that resembled a boxy office building—except for the bridge that jutted out like wings across the very top. This vacation wasn't going to be anything like the luxury cruises she'd been on before.

"Here we are," she said with a quick glance at Homicide Inspector Paavo Smith.

"Great, Angie. Super. Let's go." He was smil-

ing. Sort of. Actually, his mouth was plastered
into the same strange smile he'd worn since he
picked her up that morning.

She stared at him as he took her arm and
helped her up the steep gangway. Paavo Smith
rarely smiled, and he had never called anything super in all the time that she'd known
him. He was careful, logical, cautious, and close-
mouthed.

But then, maybe he had just decided to relax
and enjoy this cruise, their first real vacation
together. If so, that was just . . . super.

Stepping off the gangway onto the main
deck, she felt as if she'd been plunged into a
black-and-white movie. The flooring was the
color of charcoal, the walls were a grayish white,
and metallic gray paint covered everything else.
Even the ropes had a grayish cast.

Behind a gray metal table stood a tall, middle-
aged man wearing a black uniform with gold
bands on the cuffs of the jacket. A few blond
strands of hair were slicked across the top of his
head. "I am First Mate Hans Johansen," he said,
extending his hand in greeting. "Welcome to
the *Valhalla.*" His voice had a Scandinavian lilt.

"Thank you," Angie replied as Johansen gave
her and Paavo a packet of information about
the ship. He handed Paavo two sets of keys to
their cabin.

"You won't need the keys for several days,
though. We never lock our cabins while we're at
sea," Johansen stated, standing a little taller as

he spoke. "Only in port. We trust each other. That's the way of freighter life."

Angie glanced at Paavo, thinking about a pair of diamond earrings she'd brought along for nightlife in Acapulco, their destination, but he didn't notice. He continued to smile vacantly.

"You do have a safe for valuables, don't you?" she asked the first mate.

"We do," Johansen replied, his mouth taking on a wry twist. "Trust is one thing, but too much temptation is foolhardy."

A youthful steward with dark hair and deep-set, bedroomy eyes hurried over to them and stopped in front of Angie. "Allow me to show you to your cabin," he said, then picked up Angie's carry-on. He gave a cursory nod to Paavo before turning all his attention to her again. "My name is Julio Rodriguez." He clutched her bag against his heart. "I am from Chile, and I am so happy to be of service to you."

"Thank you," Angie said, taking Paavo's arm. He seemed to scarcely notice.

"Watch your step, *señorita*." Julio, walking backward, nimbly stepped over an air vent and a coil of rope. "All these hatches and vents and lines are easy to trip over."

But he didn't. She was impressed.

Sven Ingerson, the *Valhalla*'s other steward, stood on the main deck watching the freighter's few passengers check in. One hand gripped the rail, while the other pressed hard against his bilious stomach.

He'd been sick all night but hadn't said anything about it. He didn't want to be sent to a doctor or hospital and be unable to make this voyage. He needed to be on it.

He squinted against the glare of the sun. The headache he'd awakened with was growing worse by the minute, and his stomach continued to rumble.

A spasm of nausea rolled over him. The bottle of Pepto-Bismol he'd drunk hadn't helped at all. He couldn't remember ever feeling this weak or dizzy. It had to have been the pickled herring he ate yesterday, given to him by a young, pretty woman he'd met in Berkeley. When she'd offered it to him, she'd said her mother had canned it, that her mother was Norwegian—just like he was. The bitch. What had she put into the herring? Knowing Berkeley, it could have been some hallucinogen. But he wasn't feeling high. He was feeling miserable.

Maybe this was his payback for combining pleasure with the business that had taken him to Berkeley in the first place.

He wondered if it was smart not to seek medical help. But he'd never failed on a job yet. Mr. Reliable, they called him. Why not? Easy job, easy money. And he wasn't talking about being a steward.

He wiped the perspiration from his brow.

This was one job he didn't want to mess up or

be too sick to handle properly. This one was big. Just from the way the Hydra—as she was called—had talked to him about it, the way her eyes flashed as she described what he had to do, told him how important it was.

Pretending to be a street musician, singing Norwegian folk songs, was too easy to warrant the thousand dollars he was being paid. That meant there had to be a lot more to it. She thought he was too stupid to understand that. But, in fact, he understood plenty.

The whole thing was like working a thousand-piece jigsaw puzzle. He had spent many frustrating hours trying to fit all the pieces together so he could see the whole picture. He wasn't at that point yet, but he would be soon. That would be when he'd make sure he'd get a lot bigger cut than a measly thousand dollars. For all he knew, this job might even make him rich.

Then he'd never have to work for that monster again. She was called the Hydra for good reason.

Angie and Paavo followed the white uniform of the steward toward the tall deckhouse at the back of the freighter. They were within reach of it when they heard shouts behind them.

A man ran toward the railing, yanking off a white apron that circled his waist as he went and flinging it back at his pursuers. As he reached the railing and started to climb over it, several of the crewmen grabbed him, pulled him back, and wrestled him to the ground.

"What's going on?" Angie asked, watching in horrified fascination as Johansen, the first mate, with the help of the others, quickly bustled the man off the ship, down the gangway, and into the port authority building.

"That was the cook," Julio said. "He did not want to go to sea again, I guess."

"The cook?" Angie couldn't believe it. "Why was he trying to jump overboard? What's going on?"

"I think it is nothing, *señorita*," Julio said, escorting them back into the deckhouse to the elevator. "I think he is just tired of being at sea so much. It happens. We have other cooks." Julio shrugged and then hit the up button.

"But . . ." Angie turned away from Julio. "Paavo, did you see that? It was crazy."

"I saw it," he said, then shrugged in a bizarre imitation of the young steward. "It's nothing." Then he smiled at her.

She wasn't sure if it was the cook's behavior or Paavo's that was the more peculiar.

When the elevator doors slid open, they stepped into a small, utilitarian, gray-walled elevator—no carpet, no mirrors, not even Muzak. Julio pushed the button for the fourth deck.

"The cabins for passengers and officers," he said, "are on the fourth and fifth decks instead of down in the hull like on a cruise ship." He barely concealed his scorn for the competition. "Once, the cabins were all for officers, but now, since we carry the big containers, we do not need so many crew. So, we do not need so many officers. It is bad for officers but good for me," he announced with a smile. "Me and Sven Ingerson are the stewards for the passengers. You need anything, you call Julio. I will help you . . . both," he added with a quick glance at Paavo.

"Thank you," Angie said when it became clear Paavo wasn't going to respond. He had slid his hands in his pants pockets and, wearing that same, insipid smile, stared up at the elevator light that blinked with the number of the deck they were on.

On four, the elevator doors opened and they stepped out into a short hallway.

Julio hurried ahead of them and unlocked the cabin door. "Here you are," he said as he pushed it open with a flourish and waited for them to enter, then rushed past them to draw back the drapery. "Your room has big windows instead of tiny portholes, so you get lots of good light. You will see that everything is very—" His eyes met Angie's, and he swallowed hard. "—beautiful."

"Oh, my! This is lovely," Angie said. The cabin was far larger than any she'd had on a cruise ship. Maybe Paavo hadn't been as off base as she'd imagined when he pooh-poohed her suggestion to take a cruise on a big liner.

As Paavo stood, doing nothing, in the middle of the cabin, the steward padded closely after

Angie as she investigated the accommodations. In the stateroom, battleship gray was gone. Wooden shelves, a desk, and built-ins filled one side wall. Ahead, a rose-colored sofa sat below windows attractively covered with rose and white drapery. Facing the sofa was a coffee table and two green upholstered chairs. Off to the side was a separate bedroom with a closet.

"Officers lived very well here," Julio said.

"You're right," Angie agreed, stepping into the bedroom. She pushed on the mattress of the queen-size bed, testing its firmness, and mentally calculated how she and Paavo would fit on it. The bed had a raised, padded edge around it to prevent anyone from rolling off during high seas. Not to worry—she had Paavo to hold on to.

"Here's the bathroom." Julio's voice echoed from the small room off the entryway. Angie turned toward it, but he was already back in the sitting room.

"Here," he continued, looking at Paavo, "is a wall bed"—his gaze turned to Angie—"in case you want it."

Paavo didn't bat an eye.

Julio raced to the other side of the room to a small chest in the wall of built-ins and flung open a door. "You have a refrigerator and snack bar. And over there"—he darted across the room just as Angie swung open the closet door, stopping barely in time to avoid a collision—"is the closet."

"So I see," she replied. A full-length mirror

was inside the door, and she used it to smooth her dress and fluff her hair.

"Call if you need me, *señorita*," he said breathlessly, backing toward the door. He turned and pulled it open onto his foot, and left with a slight limp.

Angie noticed that Paavo was still standing in the middle of the room.

"We'll be setting sail anytime now," she said.

"Yes."

She frowned. "Paavo, is something wrong?"

He slid his hands in his pockets and walked to the window. Looking out at the harbor, he replied softly, "Everything's fine." Abruptly, he faced her. "Very fine, in fact." He crossed the cabin to the snack bar. "I thought I'd wait to tell you about it . . . but this is as good a time as ever. Let's see if they have anything in here that we can use to make this a proper celebration."

Celebration? What did he have to celebrate? Or better yet, what did *they* have to celebrate? The possibilities sent her pulse racing. "Anything will do," she said as she watched him paw through the contents of the snack bar.

"It'll have to." He stood up with a couple of cans of cola. "I'd hoped for something a little more elegant."

Angie found two glasses. "It's too early for elegant, anyway," she said, pouring the cola. "This is fine." She handed him a glass. "Now . . . as you were saying?" She couldn't contain her excitement a moment longer.

"Angie, this is something you've been thinking about for a while. Maybe even—if I've understood you—hoped for."

There was only one thing she'd been thinking about for a long time that involved Paavo—their future together. Marriage. She could scarcely speak. "Yes?"

His gaze met hers and held. "This might seem a bit sudden. But I'm sure it's the right thing to do."

She nodded with encouragement. He put his cola down on the coffee table. So did she, then stood and faced him, waiting.

"Angie, I'm leaving the police force."

She hadn't heard him right. As much as she would have been amazed had he actually proposed, this was an even bigger shock. "You can't possibly mean that."

"I do mean it. I'm quitting. When we get back from vacation, I'll make it official. I already gave Lt. Hollins notice."

She dropped onto the sofa, unable to stop staring at him. Something was wrong. That was the only logical explanation. "What happened?"

"Nothing. Being a cop, a homicide inspector, wears you down after a while. The constant brutality that you see, day in and day out. I'm tired, burned out—I'll admit it. I lasted longer than most, but it's time to try something new."

Sitting there with her mouth hanging open made her feel decidedly stupid, but she couldn't seem to shut it. To have him leave the police, the dangers of that profession, was what she'd hoped for, prayed for, from the first moment she realized she loved him. But this news was so sudden, so unexpected.

"Do you mind?" he asked.

"Mind?" She was off the sofa like a shot and took his hands. "Of course I don't mind. It's just that I never thought . . . I heard your words, but I'm finding it difficult to believe them."

"Believe them, Angie."

She studied his face, but his expression was closed to her. "Just think," he murmured. "We'll finally be able to spend more time together. Do more. Plan more. This cruise is a new beginning for us. Isn't that what you wanted?"

"Oh, yes!" She lifted her hands to his shoulders. The thought of not having to live with the constant, nagging worry about his work was like a miracle to her. An uneasiness about his sudden decision lurked just beneath the surface as she looked at him, but she pushed it aside, choosing to ignore anything that might interfere with her happiness. Squeezing her eyes tightly shut, she wrapped her arms around him and nestled her head against his neck as she replied, "It's exactly what I've wanted for a long, long time."

2

In a complex known as the Lawrence Laboratory in the hills overlooking the University of California campus in Berkeley, Professor Conrad Von Mueller slowly, methodically stroked his goatee as he, once again, pored over records of the effect of mixing 0.97 part deuterium with one part palladium. At age sixty-seven, he found it hard to believe he came here to the laboratory each day, that he wasn't home enjoying the fruits of long years of successful work and study. But he'd had no fruits of success, only long years of discouragement, faulty experiments, and bad investments.

Until now.

He slid his horn-rimmed glasses down his nose and peered over the top of them, better able to see the rows of tiny numbers. As always, the experiment had worked as he'd hoped.

While running the results through a shredder, he rubbed his eyes, then put the glasses on again. Someday he might get used to this ever-worsening eyesight, this strange combination of being both near- and farsighted, and determine whether he could see better with the wretched trifocal glasses or without them.

Maybe he needed to invent a new kind of glasses. He chuckled as he watched the last paper disappear. Soon enough he'd have the time to pursue such work.

And the money.

A knock at his office door startled him. He froze, listening. "Mail," came the softly feminine voice.

He breathed easier. "Come in, Susan," he called, a little too jovially. He'd have to watch that. He had to act the same as ever. Couldn't let anyone get suspicious.

The door opened and his graduate assistant reached into the office just far enough to drop the mail into an in-tray next to the door. "Morning, Professor," she said, giving him a warm smile.

He nodded, somewhat awkwardly, and she shut the door and was gone. A nice girl, Susan, he mused, thinking of the smile and blur of long, silky blond hair swinging seductively as she leaned into the office. He'd never been one to pay much attention to the young female grad students. Not like some of his peers, anyway.

Maybe he'd have time for that soon, too.

He smiled as he crossed the room to his tray,

despite the painful dragging of his left foot as he went, and sorted quickly through the letters. One in particular caught his attention: an oversized soft plastic mailer from UPS. He peered nervously at the return address.

Ah, Professor Luftenberg. A colleague. He gave a forced chuckle. You could never be too careful. No, you couldn't. Not with these people. He glanced fearfully toward the door again, then shook off the feeling.

He put the big envelope aside. Unbidden, his thoughts turned once again to the street musician in Berkeley, the tall blond fellow singing Norwegian songs. The contact to whom he'd passed the microfilm with his formula. He rubbed his brow. Had he made a mistake taking that route? But if he wanted to be someone, be noticed and admired for once in his life, what choice did he have?

If only he didn't have the eerie feeling that he'd been followed. Who would follow him, though? Why would anyone bother? He'd made the transfer. The deed was done. It wasn't as if he could take it back now, even if he wanted to. It was gone. Out of his hands. He'd made a deal with the woman and the big-money interests she represented. No one else was involved, so there couldn't possibly have been anyone following him. Could there?

He walked slowly back to his desk, feeling suddenly much older. Still standing, he called the special number he had been given in the

Caymans. Before long, he was put through to a banker. After giving the coded information previously agreed upon for his account, he said, "I want to make sure the denomination of the money is clearly indicated. U.S. dollars."

"Of course, Professor," the tinny voice came over the line.

"And the amount? No question about it, is there?"

"None at all, sir. The amount is five million United States dollars. It hasn't been placed in the account yet, you understand. It's still awaiting final authorization to be moved."

"That's fine. That's as it should be. I understand," he said.

Tomorrow, though, the bank's message should be quite different. If it wasn't, well . . . he had his backup plans. He was a good scientist. Even though it appeared he had destroyed his paperwork, all his formulas, as a good scientist he could always replicate his experiments.

That was what differentiated science from mere miracles.

3

Angie stood on the bridge deck at the top of the deckhouse as the *Valhalla* steamed under the steel girders of the Golden Gate Bridge toward the open sea. Although the sky over Oakland Harbor, where they'd boarded, had been clear, once they passed Alcatraz, it had turned gray and overcast with a breeze so cold she had to put on a down jacket and scarf. As the freighter nosed through the choppy waters, the faint outline of the isolated Farallon Islands in the distance gave them the appearance of rocky sentinels guarding the passage to the bay.

Although ugly containers stretching to the bow somewhat destroyed the romantic image of a tramp steamer or a slow boat to China, she wasn't about to complain. Not after what she'd gone through to get Paavo on this cruise in the first place.

She leaned forward, her elbows on the railing, her chin propped in her hands. Considering how difficult it had been to lure him away from his job, she couldn't help but wonder about his sudden decision to leave the police force altogether.

She remembered how, from the moment she'd learned he had a two-week vacation coming, her main purpose in life had been to find a way to spirit him far from his partner, his co-workers, San Francisco homicides in general, and have him all to herself. She'd been determined to find a way to make him pay sufficient attention to her that he might propose—or at least consider it.

Her plan of attack had been to move him far from any place where a murderer might lurk. A cruise ship had seemed ideal. Not many dangerous people were likely to commit murder in a spot from which there was no easy means of escape.

That decided, her first step had been to suggest an article for *Haute Cuisine* magazine, an article to be called "Dining Out in Acapulco." It was accepted. That, of course, meant she had to go to Acapulco for research. What better way to get there than by taking a cruise?

To her amazement, Paavo had flatly refused the idea. For some reason, the notion of being packed like a sardine with hundreds of strangers, plus having a social director plan his days and nights, appalled him.

But Inspector Smith hadn't considered travel

by freighter. Actually, Angie hadn't considered it either, but when she was complaining about Paavo's stubbornness to her cousin Sebastian, who knew everything there is to know about the travel business, he had said, "Angie, no problem."

The very next day he had her and Paavo booked on a Norwegian freighter bound for South America, leaving in ten days.

"Paavo, your wish is my command," she had told him that evening. He pretended he didn't know what she was talking about, so she added, "You said you would only go on a cruise if it didn't have a lot of people. I've found one for you."

"I never said I wanted to go on *any* cruise," he countered.

"Trust me," she replied with blithe confidence. "You'll love it."

He'd been involved in a homicide investigation right up until almost the time to board. Last night, she had thought she was going to have to go to his house to pack for him, but he'd made it home on time.

His case was finished. He'd found his man and arrested him, and now he should be feeling good about himself and his work.

Good enough to quit. What was wrong with this picture?

She studied him as he stood beside her, his hands gripping the cold steel railing. He was a tall man with a broad-shouldered build. His face was thin with high cheekbones, his nose slightly bent from more than one break, his mouth firm, and his eyes a sky blue color Angie found absolutely beautiful. Those eyes were now peering hard at the ocean while gusts of wind sprinkled with a fine sea mist tossed his dark brown hair askew. His mind was clearly miles away. Probably back at the Hall of Justice, mentally saying good-bye.

She reached out and placed her hand on his forearm. He glanced at her and his mouth curved into a small smile.

His eyes were bleak with weariness, though, and his shoulders slumped. Last night, after finishing work, instead of sleeping, he had probably spent the entire night packing, catching up on mail, paying bills, and—she was sure—thinking about his decision to leave, which couldn't have been easy, no matter what he said about his reasons. "Why don't you go and lie down?" she said softly. "Maybe sleep a bit?"

He shook his head and pushed back off the railing. "Once I go to sleep, I'll need more than a short nap. I don't want to miss anything. I'll get some coffee. I'll be okay. Is there anything you'd like?"

"Perrier, if they have it," she replied.

"Be right back." He gave her a quick kiss. She watched him walk down the stairs toward the deck with the passenger lounge.

"Hey there!" a woman's voice called out.

She turned to see two people behind her. The man was tall and lanky, with a wrinkled, bloodhoundlike face, fuzzy white hair in tight little curls, and on his chin a beard, scraggly in a way only very old men or as-yet-undeveloped teen boys possess. He wore a Stanford sweatshirt, Birkenstock sandals, heavy wool socks, and baggy jeans—baggy in the way of old men who have no behind to hold them up, not in the way of punk teenagers.

His companion was also dressed like an over-the-hill college student. She wore an I ♥ SEATTLE T-shirt, Calvin Klein jeans, and penny loafers. Long steel-colored hair was pulled into a knot at the top of her head, with wisps flying about her face and neck. The skin on her face was paper-thin, stretched back from a long nose that dipped down to a pointed, fleshy tip. She was the younger-looking of the two.

Angie knew that freighters that carried twelve or fewer passengers, like the *Valhalla*, weren't mandated to house a medical staff. Travel guidelines required that passengers meet a certain level of agility, plus an age limit of seventy-five or eighty years. She wondered if these two had faked their way on by trying to look younger than they were. Sort of the opposite of being carded at age twenty-one.

"Hello," Angie said, smiling. "I'm—"

"Ruby Cockburn here," the woman said. Her voice could have doubled as the ship's foghorn. "Said hey, not hello. Wondered what you were up to."

"Nothing." Angie was taken aback. "I was just looking at the view."

"Not much to see yet." Ruby waved her thumb in the old man's direction. "That's my husband, Harold."

"What?" Harold said.

Ruby jabbed his arm, and he reached out his hand to meet Angie's.

"Angelina Amalfi," she said as they shook hands.

"Odd name," Ruby said. "Are you an American?"

"Why, yes—"

"Good. Lots of foreigners on this ship. Whole crew is foreign, from what I've seen." Ruby looked over one shoulder, then the other.

"Well, it's Norwegian registry and—"

"Hope the captain knows what he's doing. Should be simple, though. Follow California south, along the coast of Baja. Then to Cabo. Harold and me, that's where we're headed. I've never been to Cabo. You been there, Miss Amala-whatever?"

"Amalfi. I've been there. Cabo San Lucas is quite nice."

"Good. You going there?"

"Not on this trip," Angie said. "My friend and I are going to Acapulco."

"This trip? You been on the *Valhalla* before?" Ruby asked.

"No. I meant, I've been to Cabo other ways before. This time, though, I'm going to Acapulco."

"But the freighter goes to Cabo San Lucas."

Ruby turned to her husband. "It goes to Cabo San Lucas, Harold. That's what we were told. Did that travel agent lie? Shifty eyes on that one." She scrutinized Angie, as if trying to determine if her eyes were shifty. "Learned that in the military. The WACs. None of this namby-pamby co-ed modern stuff."

"What?" Harold asked.

"You're okay," Angie said. "This boat will stop at Cabo and then I'll go on to Acapulco."

"Oh. So you *have* been on the *Valhalla* before," Ruby said. "Thought you said you hadn't. Make up your mind. Or you lying about it? Why? Something wrong with this boat?"

"Nothing's wrong with it, I'm sure," Angie said.

"Then why won't you admit to being on it before?"

"Okay, I'll admit it," Angie said. Why argue?

"Hello!" A tall, blond-haired steward came up to them. "You have already met, I see." He turned to Angie. "I am Sven Ingerson, at your service. You must be Miss Amalfi." She held out her hand to him and they shook.

"I am." His hand, she noticed, was fiery hot and damp.

"I'd love an iced tea, young man," Ruby said.

"Gladly," he murmured, and took out his handkerchief to dab his temple. "Would anyone else like something?"

"Mr. Ingerson," Angie said, "are you sure you're feeling well enough to be working? Why don't you sit down? You look feverish."

"I'm all right."

"I insist."

"He does look ill," Ruby said. "You got a sick bay? Think you need it, son. I'll pass on that tea. Got to get yourself shipshape."

"Go ahead," Angie urged.

"Thank you," he said with a nod. His gaze met Angie's. "You're very kind."

As Angie watched Sven leave, Paavo stepped up with her Perrier and introduced himself to the Cockburns. He was acting almost jovial. She couldn't stand it.

"Let's go to the other side of the ship and look at the pelicans," she said, taking his arm and turning him from Ruby's inquiring gaze. There were too many strange birds on this side.

4

"Sven!" The Hydra called out his name in a harsh whisper as she marched up to where he lay sprawled across three chairs placed side by side in a dark corner of the passenger lounge. Except for him, the lounge was empty. "Are you insane? What in the hell are you doing?"

He clumsily turned his head to face her. Although the grimace that twisted his lips lasted less than a second, she noticed it.

"Get up!" she ordered.

"The passengers can see I'm sick," he said with a whine. "Miss Amalfi said I should lie down."

"When *Miss Amalfi* runs this ship you can listen to her. Until then, get your butt off those chairs!" She watched him struggle to sit up, then press his arm against his forehead. Was that perspiration on his brow? Now it was all over the sleeve of his uniform. What was wrong with the man? Who would want a steward who had been sweating all over himself?

She tried to swallow her irritation as she stepped closer and spoke, her voice scarcely above a whisper. "Give me the microfilm. Quick."

"I can't."

"*What?*"

"It's in my cabin. I didn't want to carry it around. It's too valuable—right?" He stared at her.

"It's . . . it's of some value. Of course. But that's none of your business. Your job was to get it and pass it to me. Now, do your job." She hated working with fools, but they tended to take orders better than the smart ones.

"Maybe I'm not quite ready to do the job you paid me so little for," Sven said. He was sitting, his hands gripping the seat of the chair to steady himself. "Maybe that microfilm is worth a lot more than you've given me. Maybe it's time we renegotiate our deal, or I find out who else is interested in that film."

"You miserable excuse for a man! You think you can threaten me? Remember, Ingerson, you're just a steward."

"Well, you're just a—"

"Shut up, Sven! Do as I say, and without argument, or you will live to regret it, I promise you that."

"Why did the cook try to jump off the ship?" Sven asked abruptly.

"How in the hell should I know? The man was crazy. All men are. So are you. Get moving. I'll follow behind you. I want that microfilm now."

Sven opened his mouth to argue but then seemed to think better of it. His legs were shaky as he stood and crossed the lounge to the door. He had almost reached it when Angie Amalfi appeared.

"Oh, how lucky to find you," she cried. "I was just looking for some coffee. My friend is trying to keep awake, but it's a losing battle. I was hoping there might be some already made here in the lounge."

"Miss Amalfi! Uh, yes. There is usually a pot going, but it's empty now. I'll make some."

"I'll help. You still look a little peaked, I'm afraid."

"You're much too kind. But I think we—" He turned around, his hand out as if to indicate someone with him.

Behind him, the room was empty.

5

Paavo sat on a chaise longue next to
Angie's, a cup of coffee at his side, and stared
out at the ocean. He didn't have to do a single
thing if he didn't want to. It felt strange. When
Angie suggested they not bother to unpack yet,
but simply sit and talk, he had imagined it
would be easy. It wasn't. His mind raced with
what was going on back in Homicide, with what
would be happening there tomorrow, and with
all he'd been ordered to stay away from.

With all he'd decided to leave behind.

Now if he could only stop thinking about it,
he'd be fine. He had to turn his attention elsewhere. To Angie, to their future.

Once he'd understood how much their vacation together meant to her, he'd bought the
tickets himself. The cruise was his gift to her, a
gift he hoped would show her what he was so
bad at putting into words: that he loved her.

He took a deep breath and reached for her hand, feeling how delicate it was, how soft her skin was, the steady rhythm of her pulse. He lifted her hand and kissed it. Big brown eyes flashed at him and she smiled in that secret way that told him she loved him and wanted him, just as he did her. He shut his eyes, trying to relax in her glow, her warmth. Trying to unwind. Trying to forget all that he didn't like about the world.

Trying to forget that just before he had left the city, his life had gone to hell.

At the sound of approaching footsteps, he opened his eyes again. Julio Rodriguez stood before them.

"Dinner will be served soon," Rodriguez announced with a click of his heels. "Captain Olafson requests the honor of your presence at his table." He helped Angie to stand as she picked up the big tote bag she'd started carrying soon after they boarded. In it she had put her wallet, passport, sunglasses, and the myriad other things that Paavo couldn't begin to understand why she, and many other women, seemed to think they needed to cart around with them.

Julio held out his arm to Angie. "With your permission, Mr. Smith, I will help Miss Amalfi, since the ship is rolling quite a bit. *Señorita?*" The courtesy, from his lips, sounded far too much like a caress to suit Paavo. Besides, he hadn't noticed the ship swaying any more forcefully than earlier, and Angie had been able to walk just fine.

He stepped forward. "That's all right. I'll see to the lady."

Julio took one look at Paavo's expression and scurried ahead.

In the dining room, Captain Olaf Olafson greeted Angie and Paavo, a glass of vodka in his hand. Paavo noticed that it didn't appear to be his first. The captain's cheeks were flushed and his eyes overly bright. He wore a black uniform that fit a bit too snugly, with slightly bedraggled gold epaulets.

Julio introduced them, then seated Angie and Paavo at the table, with Angie on the captain's right. The room was surprisingly small and cozy, with one large round table covered with a white cloth and set with white china. The crew ate in a separate mess. Already seated at the captain's table were Ruby and Harold Cockburn.

"I shall introduce your traveling companions, *ja?*" Captain Olafson said grandly, waving his vodka glass at a couple across the table. They greeted the Cockburns, then the captain turned to another couple who had just entered the dining room.

"This is Mr. and Mrs. Marvin Nebler, also from the U.S. of A. I have the honor to introduce Miss Angelina Amalfi and her companion, Mr. Paavo Smith." Paavo stood to greet them.

This couple, too, was clearly pushing the age limit.

"I'm Nellie." Mrs. Neblar held out her hand to them. She was wearing a yellow and green flo-

ral print blouse with starched yellow Bermuda
shorts, rolled bobby socks, and white sneakers.
Ghost-white arms and legs jutted from the
clothes.

On her head she wore a big, bouffant, golden
blond wig with the hair shellacked into place.

"How nice to meet you," Angie and Paavo
said.

Her husband spoke. "I'm Marvin, once Marvy
Marv of automobile fame."

"Really?" Angie said. Marvy Marv was a short,
round man, with thin wisps of dyed reddish
brown hair and beady brown eyes. Angie tried
not to stare at his hair, but the color and texture
looked a lot more like the result of shoe polish
than of Grecian Formula. His loud red and
white Hawaiian shirt was fashionably unironed,
as opposed to Nellie's starched Bermudas, but
with it he wore dark brown gabardine trousers—
the sort usually found as part of a suit.

"Yes. '*Buy the best used cars from Marvy Marv,
Burlingame and South San Francisco.*' I'm sure
you've heard that radio commercial."

"I'm sure," she said. Sure she hadn't, but who
was counting? "How do you do?" Angie held out
her hand to Marvy Marv himself.

He stared at it, as if unsure what to do with it,
then gave her and Paavo a quick shake before
stuffing his thick hands into his pockets.

She sneaked a glance at her hand, wondering
what he'd found so objectionable. He was a
used-car salesman if ever she saw one. Except

for the handshake. Maybe that's what used car
salesmen did when they retired—they stopped
shaking hands.

As they sat, Marvy Marv caught her eye and
said, "Ruby Cockburn told us you're the expert
on this ship."

"I'm not an expert—"

"She's lying again," Ruby announced. "You've
got to watch her. She's been on this ship a lot.
Knows the whole itinerary. But she likes to keep
it to herself." She gave Angie a hard stare. "Soldiers were court-martialed for less in my day."

"There's been a misunderstanding, I'm afraid,"
Angie said. She glanced at Paavo, expecting to
see some reaction from him, some defense of
her honor, but he sat there smiling pleasantly at
the group.

All this smiling was starting to get on her
nerves.

Just then, Johansen, the first mate, joined
them with apologies for being late.

Soon wine was poured, and the meal was
served.

Captain Olafson stood, holding a wineglass in
the air. "This is a goot day for the *Valhalla,* bringing us so many fine people to be our guests. I
propose a toast to your goot health."

They all raised their glasses, and soon the typ-
ical small talk and light laughter of a dinner
party began.

The meal was uninspired—roasted chicken,
mashed potatoes, vegetables, and peach tart for

dessert. Compared to the lavish meals Angie had had on other cruises she'd taken, this was a definite downside to freighter travel.

"So, Miss Amalfi," Captain Olafson said. "Tell us about yourself. What brings you to the *Valhalla?*"

She met Paavo's gaze and held it, as if to remind him, as she answered. "Paavo and I are here for a long-awaited vacation."

"What do you do in San Francisco?"

The question sliced through her. "What do I . . . *do?*" This was a sore point. As much as she had tried to find an interesting, important, and well-paying job, nothing had worked out the way she'd expected. She'd been a newspaper columnist, a talk radio assistant, a culinary adviser for an inn, and a chocolatier, and she had even tried her hand at TV. Each had failed.

She did have her assignment for *Haute Cuisine* magazine, though—it'd pay all of three hundred dollars, if and when it ever got published. She decided to ignore the time and expense of getting to Acapulco and paying for big meals in a number of fine restaurants. "I'm a restaurant reviewer," she announced. "An *international* restaurant reviewer, in fact." She could lay it on as thick as the best of them.

"Ah!" the captain cried. "I must warn our cooks to do well or they will find themselves with the black mark. Maybe zero forks, *ja?*"

"This dinner is very nicely prepared," Angie said, then added, "For simple, basic food. It's good someone else was able to take over after what happened to the cook . . . whatever it was." It would be impolite to come out and *ask*, even if she were dying of curiosity.

"That's so sweet," Nellie interjected. "To write lovely articles for wonderful magazines."

"When I buy a magazine, it ain't for the articles," Marvy Marv said, waggling his eyebrows.

"Marvin, really!" Nellie said.

Angie tried again. "Captain Olafson, about the cook—"

"Never did cook much myself," Ruby said, pushing around a piece of peach that seemed to be sticking to her plate. "I let the boys assigned to KP do it. I had *real* work to do. Anyway, she doesn't look like a cook to me. Too skinny."

"I think Miss Amalfi looks just right," Olafson announced with a self-satisfied smile, as if pleased over his charming ways with women. "And you, Mr. Smith. Do you work?"

He caught Paavo in the middle of a yawn.

"Paavo's a hom—"

He squeezed her hand—tightly—stopping her words. "I work for city government," he said with a smile. "Just a bureaucrat."

Angie stared at him. He'd been practically comatose since the meal started, and now awoke to call himself a bureaucrat? And to smile about it? Was this the new Paavo?

"I don't believe he's telling the truth, either," Ruby announced.

Paavo gawked at her.

"He looks too tired to be one of those people," she said. "They just sleep on the job. Right, Harold?" She prodded her husband.

"Huh?" he said.

"Harold used to work for the Department of Education," she said, then shouted. "Know all their tricks, don't we, Harold?"

Captain Olafson chuckled. "Ah! No wonder Mr. Smith wanted to ride on our big boat. The bureaucrat's life is very dull, *ja?*"

Paavo nodded and smiled.

Angie gave up trying to talk to any of them. Including Paavo.

As soon as Marvin finished his last bite of dessert, he announced it was his bedtime, although it wasn't even seven o'clock yet.

"Oh, my, this has all been so fascinating," Nellie cried as she stood up. "It's all so very . . . cosmopolitan. Good night, dearies," she said to Angie and Paavo. Then she turned to Marvin and added, "Young love is so sweet!"

Angie's eyes jumped to Paavo, expecting to see him cringe.

To her amazement, not only was he nodding and smiling that smile she was growing really sick of, but he was wishing them pleasant dreams as well.

6

Professor Von Mueller looked at the big clock over his desk. Eight o'clock. He really should be thinking about going home. But what did home offer him? He thought of the small, sterile apartment. Nothing. Soon, though . . .

A villa along the Riviera would be nice. He'd always wanted one. Or maybe something smaller, like an apartment in Venice. On the Grand Canal.

He got up, put his flat brown cap on his head, took his cane in hand, and hobbled toward the door. He was about to shut off the light and leave when his eye caught his unopened mail. It couldn't be anything that would interest a man soon to possess five million dollars, but nonetheless, he had some curiosity about it.

He took off the hat and sat down at his desk, listening to the creaking of his joints as he did so. Adjusting his glasses, he picked up the large envelope from his colleague and studied the address once more. He hadn't heard from Professor Luftenberg in years. In fact, it seemed he'd been told the man had died. Obviously, his memory was faulty in that area.

Not in all areas, though. Not where it mattered. He thought once more about his discovery. About his formula.

He tried yanking the envelope open, but it was one of those self-stick Tyrek packets. He soon gave up and grabbed a pair of scissors. This was truly a wonder product. How something so light and simple could be so airtight and strong was quite amazing. He almost wished he'd invented it, but then dismissed the idea.

A man who had come up with the discovery that would revolutionize the world, would change the future of mankind, had no business wasting his time with packaging material.

Whistling tunelessly, he cut the envelope. When he pulled it open, a puff of powder billowed out at him, tickling his nose. He sneezed, then drew in his breath and sneezed again. As the powder settled into his mouth and lungs from his deep inhale, he began to feel a tingling sensation, then nothing.

His mouth, his nose, his tongue turned numb, then grew paralyzed. Panicking, he opened his mouth, trying to speak, to cry out for help. No sound came. His tongue seemed to slide back into his throat, cutting off his air. He clawed at his mouth, his fingers reaching deep into the back of his throat as he pressed his tongue out of the way.

But his lungs wouldn't work; they wouldn't inhale. He was suffocating . . . and he knew it.

His arm hit the cane, knocking it aside as he stumbled toward the door. His glasses fell from his face. He could scarcely see. Where was his grad student? His helper? *Susan!* His mind shrieked for her, but his voice was still. He needed air, needed to breathe.

He reached the door, and yanked it open.

The hallway was empty. No one, no help . . . He stepped into the hall and fell to his knees, then onto his back. *Susan!*

The only movement on his face was a single tear that rolled down his wrinkled cheek.

7

"Sven! You bastard, I've been looking for you all night."

He cringed. The Hydra. He wished she were dead.

He was curled up on a deck chair, covered by a blanket. He no longer felt nauseous; instead the pains in his stomach were so bad he couldn't even drink water. His legs and arms had turned almost numb, and now this monster was yelling at him. He'd thought he'd be safe from her up here on the bridge deck. Passengers came up here only to watch the freighter sail into and out of harbors, but their next stop wasn't until Cabo San Lucas. "I'm trying to get a little peace and quiet," he whispered. It hurt to talk. "I'm sick. And sick of everyone hassling me."

"And I'm sick of you and your whining." Her contorted face pressed close to his. If he'd brought a knife, she'd be fish food.

"Give me the microfilm and be quick about it," she demanded. "I don't want anyone to see us together."

The microfilm. That was all she cared about. Not him, not his illness. "I can't."

"Now what? What did you do with it, you fool? I swear you'll never work for me again. Do you hear me?"

He rubbed his forehead. The microfilm was in his pocket. He could give it to her and be done with her and her temper. But then she'd win and he'd lose. "I wasn't able to go get it yet. I've been too sick."

"I don't believe this! Sometimes I wonder why I bother with you at all. You are so worthless." She paced around. "Listen, too many other crewmen will be milling around your quarters this time of night. I'd better not go with you to get it. The first chance you get, I want you to bring it to the galley. Anyone can go in there day or night for a soft drink or a snack, so it won't look suspicious. I'll be waiting for you, but if I'm not there for some reason—or if someone else is and you can't pass it to me—put it in an open sack of sugar."

"Sugar?"

"No, wait—if any water or perspiration got on it, it might get sticky, and that might ruin it."

"I don't want to be around food." He groaned.

"I've got it. Put it in a tin of baking powder. It'll stay dry, and no one will pick it up and use it by chance. I don't think we have anyone who'll want to bake while on board."

"I'm too sick." He started to lie down again. "I can't go down there."

She grabbed his shirt with both hands and yanked him upright, her face only inches from his. "Your cabin is down there! If you didn't leave the microfilm—" She stopped and looked around. She must have realized how loud her voice had become. "If you hadn't left it in your cabin, none of this would have happened! You'll go to your cabin, get the microfilm, and bring it to the galley. If I'm not there, put it in the open tin of baking powder. Is that clear?"

He nodded sullenly, unwilling to let her see his fear.

"Do it tonight," she ordered.

A stabbing pain hit his stomach so fiercely he doubled over, clutching it and moaning. She let go of him and jumped back, as if afraid he'd contaminate her.

"Remember—baking powder. Hide it in the baking powder."

"I heard you." He could barely speak.

"And hurry up! I don't want you to die before you've put it where I can find it." She headed for the stairs.

"Slut," he murmured as he watched her go.

In her cabin, Angie took a bottle of vintage port and two stemmed glasses from a padded and lined wine-bottle carrying case she'd bought in the Napa Valley. She'd been warned ahead of time by her cousin Sebastian that on a freighter everything was bare bones and generic, so if you wanted any special treats, you had to bring them yourself. She had brought a bottle of white wine, one of a vintage port, and one of champagne, plus fancy stemmed glasses to drink them out of. She had planned to spend some romantic evenings with Paavo on this cruise, even if she had to set them up herself. But now they had a big reason to celebrate.

She was sure she'd get used to Paavo the civilian, smiling and friendly around strangers, rather than Paavo the cop, who was constantly serious and cautious. The change was a shock to her, but a welcome one.

She put on a heavy jacket, as did Paavo, and, leaving everything else behind, they carried the port and the glasses from the cabin down the hallway to the small outdoor area on the fourth deck.

As she stepped out the door, she saw the blond steward leaning heavily against the rail.

"Sorry," he mumbled, then, swaying slightly, headed for the door she and Paavo had just stepped through. He seemed to have trouble finding the door handle, but he finally made it into the hallway.

Frowning, Angie stared after him a moment. When he didn't come back out, she guessed he was all right. Being ill, he must have decided to take the slow elevator to his room instead of the stairs, the way most people did.

Turning her thoughts from the sick man, she

poured some port into each glass, then handed one to Paavo.

"*Salute,*" she said.

"To us," Paavo responded. "And to our future," he added meaningfully.

They clinked their glasses together, her gaze locking with his as she took her first sip. Los Angeles might have been out there somewhere, but she couldn't see it and didn't even care to search. All she cared to look at was before her.

Moments later, the door to the deckhouse banged open and, wraithlike, Sven Ingerson appeared. He was gasping for breath and his face had a greenish tinge. "I can't. . . ."

They ran over to him, each taking an arm. "You need to sit down," Angie said.

"No. My cabin . . ." Ingerson swayed slightly as he rubbed his forehead. He seemed to have trouble focusing. "I did . . . powder . . . powder . . . I can't . . ."

"Powder? Medicine? Is that it?" Paavo asked. "Do you need some medicine?"

"Yes, medi . . . God, my head!"

"Angie, let's get him to the chair," Paavo said, leading Sven toward the chairs they had been using.

"No!" He lunged for the railing, clutching it tightly as he started mumbling incoherently— but it was probably Norwegian, because it didn't make any sense at all.

"He needs a hospital," Angie said, now really worried about him. He seemed out of his head.

"No! No hospital," he cried, leaning over the railing, pushing it hard against his stomach.

"Let's get him away from this railing," Paavo said, "then I'll go get help."

Angie nodded. "Please," she said gently to Sven, trying not to upset him any further. "Let me help you to the chair. You need to sit. Or, even better, you can lie down in our cabin. It's just down the hall."

"No, no, no. Mr. Reliable. Tell them . . ." Then he cried out in pain and dropped at her feet.

"My God!" Angie cried.

Paavo swiftly kneeled at the man's side and lifted his eyelids. "He's passed out. Go find the captain or first mate quick." He began loosening Sven's collar.

Angie ran up the stairs toward the bridge deck, where she hoped to find someone in charge. As she reached the sixth deck, she saw Julio at the top of the stairs. "Julio! Thank God! Get help. Mr. Ingerson, the steward, just passed out. He's on the fourth deck."

Julio ran down the flight of stairs and grabbed her hand. "Never fear, *señorita*. I will find someone for you." He turned, stumbled over a post that held up the stair railing, then ran back upstairs to the bridge and pilot house.

In no time, Captain Olafson burst out of the pilot house and hurried down the stairs. Angie directed him to the fourth deck. Other crewmen, drawn by the commotion, had already gathered. Olafson's eyes widened when he saw

Paavo bending over the steward. He turned back to Angie who had followed behind him. "What's wrong with him?" he whispered.

"I don't know," Angie said.

He stepped a bit closer to Paavo, giving a cursory glance at the unmoving steward. "How is he?"

"Scarcely breathing," Paavo said, "and burning up with fever. He needs a doctor."

The captain backed up. "Do you think it's contagious?"

Mr. Johansen, the first mate, ran over to them and knelt at Ingerson's side with a medical kit.

"I'm a trained medic," he announced. "I can handle this." But he soon realized he could do nothing to help the steward but apply cold compresses. "We'll have to dock," he said to Captain Olafson.

"But we can't." Olafson was wringing his hands.

"What do you mean, you can't?" Angie asked. "The man needs help."

"We're foreign registry. We can only dock once at a U.S. port between foreign ports— that's U.S. law."

"We have no choice," Johansen said. "We've got a serious medical emergency." He ordered two of the crewmen to carry Ingerson to his cabin, then turned back to the captain. "You've got to get on the radio and explain to Long Beach that we need to come into port. The man might die otherwise."

Olafson, now also looking pale and shaky, most likely because of the thought of dealing with U.S. authorities, began nodding moments before the word "*ja*" emerged reluctantly from his lips.

As the officers went up to the bridge, and the other crewmen dispersed, Angie and Paavo were left alone on the deck once more.

"If there's any problem with the port authorities letting the ship dock," Angie said, "maybe you could contact the LAPD and get some names of higher-ups to talk to. Sometimes a little political clout is needed in cases like this."

Paavo frowned as he stood at the rail and stared at the night lights of Los Angeles, a whitish glow on the horizon. He took a deep breath. As he exhaled, his frown disappeared and a small smile formed. "No need, Angie. I'm sure the captain will take care of everything."

That answer was nothing like Paavo. In times of trouble, or when people were in need of help, he was always there doing his best. "But what if he can't?" Angie said. "The captain's got the spine of a jellyfish. And besides, who knows what's wrong with Ingerson!"

"It's none of our business, Angie. No one else is stepping in. The Neblars and Cockburns are probably already asleep. That's what we should be doing—sleeping."

Sleep? When a man was sick? Maybe dying? This blasé, uninterested person was not Paavo.

"What if the captain was right and he's conta-

gious?" she asked, not about to give up. Then a
new thought came to her—one she was sure
would ignite Paavo's curiosity. "What if whatever
is wrong with him is something the cook knew
about, and that's why he wanted off the ship?"

He leaned back against the rail, his tone one
of relaxed insouciance. "If anything's wrong,
the proper authorities will take care of it.
Johansen is clearly a man who can take charge
and see that whatever's necessary is done. It
doesn't concern us, Angie." He smiled again.
"We're on vacation."

The Hydra sneaked into the galley and tiptoed
over to the baking powder. She wanted the
microfilm safely in her possession before anything else strange happened on this ship. There
was something about this trip that was making
her nervous.

She reached for an open tin of baking powder and dug around in it, expecting to easily
find the microfilm. She didn't. She dumped the
contents onto the counter and spread it around.
No microfilm.

She reached for a box of baking soda. What
did Sven know about cooking, anyway? To him,
they were probably the same.

But it didn't contain the microfilm either.

Before long, she'd pulled every open box, tin,
and sack of flour, sugar, oatmeal, salt, spices,
and even corn flakes off the shelf, dumped their
contents onto the counter, and sifted through

them. The microfilm still wasn't anywhere to be seen.

Her face and arms were covered with flour. She dumped the open food into garbage bags, then took a dish cloth and wiped off any traces from herself.

She was furious. So furious she couldn't think of anything except emptying an automatic into Sven Ingerson's lying, lazy body. Where in the hell had he put the microfilm? It wasn't that small. Not a microdot, thank God, which could have been anywhere. She'd told the professor to leave the film about a half inch in size—small enough to easily hide, but not lose.

So much for planning.

If it wasn't in the galley, it must still be in Ingerson's quarters.

Or . . . he had been on the fourth deck when he passed out. Angie Amalfi's room was on the fourth deck. Ingerson liked her.

No, she decided. He wouldn't have dared.

8

Just below the Tropic of Cancer, high in the mountains overlooking Mazatlán, on the Pacific coast of Mexico, a high pink wall snaked around a compound, topped by electrified barbed wire and circled by a wide treeless swathe patrolled by surveillance cameras.

Inside the compound, a hacienda sprawled like a fleshy hand clutching the mountainous perch. Its walls were adobe and rock from the hillside, too thick to be penetrated by any bullet.

Each room of the hacienda was crammed with lavish yet gaudy furniture. In the massive living room the amount of gilt and brocade was blinding. Replicas of famous artworks covered the walls. Even the bulletproof glass windows that looked out over the mountains to the jungle far away were adorned with tasseled gold-and-red velvet draperies.

Gazing out of those windows at the moonlit sky was a man with wavy black hair, graying at the temples. He was wearing a short-sleeved white shirt and black cotton slacks. A dab of blood from where he had cut himself shaving that morning stained the unbuttoned shirt collar. He was tall and barrel-chested, and stood with his shoulders squared, his chin high.

"I am at peace here, *amigo*," Colonel Hector Ortega announced, his eyes never leaving the view. "I feel like God has reached down and touched this house, this land, for me alone. Here, finally, all I have worked for throughout my life, all I have wanted to achieve, will be mine." He turned and smiled, his long, thick-jowled, and baggy-eyed face suddenly soft and wistful.

His friend and confidant, Eduardo Catalán, nearly choked on his scotch and water. "Yes, my colonel," he said, struggling to talk despite the burning in his throat. "Everything will be most splendid for you."

Catalán was as tall as the colonel, but thin and wiry where the colonel was round and sluggish. Even his gray hair was wiry; he kept it closely cropped in a stylish razor cut. His gray silk suit was handmade on Savile Row, his white shirt and tie Dior, and his shoes Gucci. He tugged at his slacks as he crossed one leg over the other.

Ortega lifted his head even higher, one hand fisted and pressed against the back of his waist as he strutted before the glass-covered wall. As if he were a real colonel, Eduardo thought, drinking more scotch to kill the ever-bitter taste in his mouth.

The colonel stopped before a statue of the Virgin Mary in the corner of the room and lit the votive candle in front of it. "This is to light the way for the woman who is bringing me my dream, even as we speak." His eyes were bright as they again faced Eduardo. "The ship has sailed now. What she brings me is worth more than anyone could imagine, even in their wildest dreams. Only a handful of us know it exists. But soon, the whole world will know. And it will be mine."

He peered hard at Eduardo. "Then my enemies will discover, finally, just how small and stupid they truly were. Everyone else will realize as well, which will be the ultimate revenge. They blocked my promotion to general when I deserved to be one! Everyone said so! But they stopped me. Soon, though, they will all come groveling at my feet."

He took out a cigar and carefully cut off the tip, tamping the tobacco, before putting it to his lips and lighting it.

"*Generale?* Hah! I spit on their offer! I will be bigger than that. Bigger than *el presidente.* I will be the one who tells *el presidente* what to do."

"Yes, my colonel," Eduardo said, making sure he sounded undeniably sincere.

9

By ten in the morning, Angie was lying on a lounge chair on the main deck in a white Ann Taylor linen sundress and Liz Claiborne straw hat, with a pair of Armani sunglasses shielding her eyes, a dab of sunscreen on her nose. She'd missed breakfast. It was served at some ungodly hour, like seven-thirty or eight. She didn't see any of the other passengers, and the few crewmen she saw working didn't appear to speak English.

So she'd gathered her belongings and decided to sunbathe. She was watching a school of porpoises not far from the ship and pondering the abruptness of Paavo's decision to quit his job when he joined her.

He sat in a lounge chair and unfolded a copy of that morning's *Los Angeles Times.*

"Where did that come from?" she asked.

"A few copies were left in the passenger lounge, along with *USA Today.*"

The Times looked thick enough to keep Paavo occupied for half the trip. "Did you hear anything about the steward?" she asked.

"He was taken to an emergency room. That's the last anyone knows."

"They just left him there?"

"Apparently." For all Paavo's interest, he could have been discussing the weather.

The ship was now heading toward Baja California without one of its stewards. The whole thing seemed rather heartless to her, but if no one else cared, she shouldn't let it bother her. Next stop, Cabo San Lucas.

With more than a little pique, Angie reached into the big tote bag she'd been filling with more and more essentials as the trip continued. She took out the latest novel she was reading. Hemingway. In the past, she'd never appreciated his books much, she was sorry to say, but a cruise seemed a good place to do some serious reading—and to impress Paavo while she was at it.

Before opening the book, though, she stole a quick glance at the newspaper headlines. She was already missing the *San Francisco Chronicle*, laden with gossip about politicians and society people—who, in San Francisco, were generally one and the same. Nothing in the more serious *Times* caught her attention. Paavo had told her they needed to leave the real world behind them. But now, as he pored over this great sea of newsprint, he didn't seem to be applying that philosophy to himself.

"Any news stories about San Francisco?" she asked.

"We've been gone only one day," Paavo said. "What could have happened? Wait, here's something."

She leaned forward with interest. "Oh?" Was it about the recent furor over one of the Forty-Niners dating a member of the board of supervisors, or maybe the escapades of a married judge and an equally married, well-known pop singer?

"A chemist from the Lawrence Lab, Dr. Conrad Von Mueller, was found dead in his office."

"A murder." She eased herself back against the sofa and opened her book. "I should have known."

"Maybe not. The paper doesn't say what he died from. But the story being in the news implies he didn't die of natural causes."

"Pardon me. I couldn't help overhearing. Someone is dead?" The question, asked in an upper-crust British accent, cut into their conversation.

Angie gazed up and up at a mountain of a man. The most striking thing about him was his huge head, its bald crown shining and bulbous, circled by a fringe of thinning gray hair. His lower face bulged out into flabby, red-veined cheeks, followed by jowls extending almost to his chest and rendering his neck a long-ago memory.

His chest rolled onto a massive stomach, over which he wore a vest with a pocket watch. His white suit jacket was open, hanging loosely on either side of his paunch, its buttons and buttonholes strangers. In his hand was a white Panama hat.

"We were talking about a newspaper article," Angie said, curious about the newcomer. "My name is Angelina Amalfi, and this is Paavo Smith."

"Charmed, madam. And Mr. Smith. Ah, such a relief that it was just a story," the Englishman said. "I've been informed that a steward was taken ill on board. It wasn't the food, was it?"

"No one else is sick, so I wouldn't worry about the food," Angie said. "And you are . . . ?"

"Oh, my!" the Englishman cried. "Pardon my bad manners! I just joined you last night. My name is Dudley Livingstone. I'm a collector. South American artifacts, to be precise."

They shook hands.

"Did you board in Long Beach?" Angie said. "I didn't realize we were taking on more passengers."

"I was quite fortunate." Livingstone eased his great bulk into a metal deck chair beside them. Angie watched the chair legs bow slightly. "The ship I was supposed to have been on left three days early, and I missed it. I'd been spending the past twenty-four hours berating the Los Angeles port authority when they got word about the emergency on this ship. Since the *Valhalla* is going to Chile, which is where I'm headed, the harbormaster arranged for me to get on."

"You were lucky," Angie said. "We weren't supposed to stop there."

"So I understand." Livingstone folded his hands over his round belly. "So, do tell me, are you going far? All the way to South America, or will this be a short jaunt?"

"We'll be leaving the ship in Acapulco," Angie answered.

"A beautiful city. One of my favorites," Livingstone said. "What about the others? Do you know?"

"One couple disembarks at Cabo San Lucas, I believe. I'm not sure about the other. How long will it take you to get to Chile?"

"Nearly two weeks, I expect, with all the stopovers along the way—which is, of course, the joy of freighter travel," he said. "I do hope I'll have some companions beside the crew. But anyway, back to the newspaper article. It sounded rather interesting. Who did you say was dead?"

"Some professor from the Lawrence Lab," Paavo answered. "Conrad Von Mueller."

Livingstone's gaze darted from one to the other. "Von Mueller! He's very famous. I can't believe it. Surely you are both aware of his work?"

"No." Paavo glanced at Angie. She shook her head. "What was his work?"

Livingstone eyed them both carefully. "Oh, a little of this and a tad of that. Chemistry, you know. Since you were talking about him, I had naturally assumed . . ." He let his voice trail off.

"You can tell us about him," Angie said.

"Why bore young people with talk of old scientists?" Livingstone stood. "It was a pleasure meeting you, Miss Amalfi." He placed his hat on his head. "And you, Mr. Smith. I look forward to conversing with you much more in the future."

As soon as Livingstone left, she turned to Paavo.

"So tell me," she said, leaning forward, "what did you think of him?"

Paavo was already scanning the newspaper again, looking for an article to catch his attention. "What do you mean?" he asked.

She gazed at the paper, then at him. The urge to jump up and shake him was overwhelming. What was wrong with him? "I didn't believe a word that man uttered! Did you?"

Paavo buried his nose deeper into the news. "Why shouldn't I?"

"Because it was so phony, as you well know!" That settled it. Something was definitely wrong with her inspector. He was usually the one to point out such things to her, not the other way around. She could handle his changing jobs— in fact, this particular change she welcomed— but a personality change along with it was beyond the pale.

She lowered her voice and kept talking. "People don't just get on board container ships at the last minute. And his interest in Von Mueller was most peculiar."

Blue eyes caught hers a moment; then Paavo gave a slight shake of his head and turned back to his paper. He flipped to another page. "Strangers have to talk about something to each other. Why not the news?"

"It wasn't that kind of chitchat," Angie said. "Tell me the truth. Didn't his questions—his whole manner—strike you as a little bit curious?"

His jaw worked a moment. "He seemed eccentric, I'll go that far."

"Aha! You did notice." What was she doing? Why was she prodding him to question the people around them? She should be glad he wasn't interested.

"It doesn't mean a thing," he added.

She gave up. She needed to change the subject, because this one was too frustrating. "By the way, what were you looking for in the bathroom cabinet?"

He put the paper down and gave her a strange look. "Now what are you talking about?" He had a long-suffering tone that she didn't much care for.

"Last night I noticed the toiletries were jumbled. I assumed you were looking for something of mine. I wondered what it was, that's all."

"I didn't touch anything of yours in the bathroom cabinet," he said firmly.

"Well, somebody did. Are you sure?"

He just looked at her.

"Well, they were jumbled together. I wonder what it means?"

Picking up the newspaper once more, he snapped the page open then folded it back. "It probably means no more than that we hit a big wave and everything slid." He lifted the paper high and continued reading.

She was ready to toss the *Times* overboard.

"I don't know why you're acting this way, Angie," Paavo said with a measured lack of interest. "Enjoy your vacation."

"Are you enjoying it?" she asked.

"Of course," he said. "Can't you tell?"

10

Later that morning, as the freighter slowly headed southward along the coast of Baja California, Angie stretched out on a lounge chair on the sundeck in a red bikini. She ignored the fact that the crew, who normally almost never appeared in the passenger areas, seemed to suddenly find all kinds of reasons to walk by.

She had decided that she shouldn't be pointing out oddities about this trip to Paavo. He was doing the right thing by ignoring them. That was what he'd do in his new persona: learn how not to be a cop. It wasn't being dull—it was being an everyday kind of guy.

Oh, well. She situated herself so that her head and shoulders were shaded by the big umbrella that rose from a round patio table. The umbrella could be angled wherever needed.

She kicked off her sandals so that her feet,

with their fuchsia-colored toenails, would tan without strap lines. Next, she picked up the book her sister Francesca had recommended to her, but she doubted she'd make it past chapter two. She didn't need a book to tell her that she and Paavo were on totally different planets.

As she glanced over at Paavo, the big umbrella shading her creaked and bent at the center joint, allowing the sun to hit her full in the face. When she put her hand up to shade her eyes, she could see he was zipping through an old Ross Macdonald mystery he'd found in the passenger lounge. She had to admit his book looked interesting. She put hers down.

"You know," she began as she stood up and pushed the umbrella back upright so that it shaded her once again.

"Hmm?" He kept reading. He was getting close to the end. Maybe she shouldn't bother him?

She stretched out on the chaise longue once more. "Am I disturbing you?"

"Not at all." He kept reading. Obviously, he'd given her an honest answer.

"Have you given any thought to what you'll do after leaving the police force?"

"Not yet. Something will turn up. Maybe I'll join the merchant marines and ship out. I could learn to enjoy a life at sea."

"You're kidding me."

He didn't say yes . . . or no. "If nothing else," he added, "I could always apply for a private eye license."

"Hmm." Somehow he didn't seem like the *Magnum, P.I.* type. He was more *NYPD Blue* material.

"I've been giving a lot of thought to my own career as well," she said after a while. The umbrella creaked and inched downward. She looked up. It stopped moving.

"Oh?" At least he didn't say, "What career?"

"I know a lot about cooking..." The umbrella creaked again.

"Yes..."

"I thought it was time to put that knowledge to good use. I should write a cookbook." The umbrella suddenly tilted so far to one side she was completely in the sun.

"That sounds like a good idea," he said without looking up.

"The problem is," she said, getting up once more to lift the umbrella back into place, "what kind of cookbook? I mean, there are all kinds out there now. Ethnic cookbooks, special diet cookbooks, single-food cookbooks—you can even get books on ways to cook parsley if you look hard enough. I mean, who cares? It's not anything to build a meal around."

He put down his book. "I guess not."

She twisted the umbrella, tugging on and tightening any screws and handles she could find, until she was sure it wouldn't move again. "I need a different angle." She flung herself back on the chaise longue. "Not food, not ethnic, not low calorie, low fat or any other diet-

related book. Something new, something different—something that'll make people throw
down their money! But what?"

"I don't know."

She frowned at him.

"What about," he began, racking his brain in
the face of her unhappiness, "a cookbook for
people who don't cook, like me? A no-cooking
cookbook?"

She heaved a big sigh—both because she was
glad to have fixed the umbrella and because of
the weightiness of her career problems. "I doubt
many people who don't cook will want to buy a
cookbook reminding them of that fact."

"You may be right," he admitted.

"I'm afraid so. But that's not a bad
approach—a style-of-cooking cookbook. Let's
see. Microwave ovens already have plenty of
cookbooks. Same with crockpots. Toaster ovens?
Not very interesting recipes. On the other hand,
I haven't seen many cookbooks on using a convection oven."

"I've never heard of a convection oven."

"They're quite popular."

"If you say so."

The umbrella suddenly flopped so far over, it
was almost upside down. Angie jumped to her
feet. She was going to tie the blasted thing in
place—if she could find something to tie it with.
"Maybe that's why there aren't a lot of cookbooks about using them. Or maybe it's easy to
just adjust a regular recipe, so no one needs a

special cookbook. What we need is something simple, but not too simple."

"Er . . . right. You'll come up with a good idea, I'm sure. Give it time." He picked up his book again.

A small chest with some ropes and tools was fixed to a nearby bulkhead. She rummaged through it and found exactly what she needed— a roll of nylon line, almost like that used on a fishing pole. Nellie and Marvy Marv put down their magazines and watched her.

"A new kind of oven," she called to Paavo as she pulled the line from the chest. "A new kind of heat. You know, they're doing all this stuff to save on fossil fuel, but what's the best kind of heat to cook with? Gas. But gas is a depletable substance. That means we've got to find something else."

She tied one end of the line to the umbrella pole that kept bending in the wrong direction, pulled the umbrella upright, then anchored the line by tying it to a metal ring sunk in the deck. It wasn't easy to see, so she'd have to find something colorful to tie on the line so that no one would trip over it. "A new source of heat . . . of energy."

"I don't think gas will be depleted in any amount of time we need to worry about." Paavo turned a page.

"That might be true, but you've got to do more than think about the here and now." She looked at the umbrella. Finally it seemed secure. "On the other hand, if you were a father . . ." Suddenly the thought of Paavo as a father to her children made her skin feel even hotter. He'd make a wonderful father, a wonderful husband. She forced her attention back to making sure the umbrella was angled properly. It seemed to be.

"If you were a father," she said, doing all she could to keep her voice steady, "you'd worry more about the future."

Ruby Cockburn stepped onto the deck. She was going to say something when she caught Angie's last words. She snapped her jaw shut.

"What?" Harold asked.

She jabbed his ribs to silence him. "S-e-x," she mouthed, then pointed at Angie and Paavo. He nodded and they moved closer.

"If I were a father," Paavo said, "my number one worry would be how to stop your father from killing me."

Angie could hear the smile in his voice. She could have pointed out that if certain legalities were observed, her father would have no objection at all to her carrying Paavo's child . . . except for the fact that Sal Amalfi didn't like him one little bit.

But what was a family without a few members who couldn't stand each other?

"That's probably true," she said finally. All in all, maybe this wasn't the time to get into a conversation with more ramifications to it than she was ready to deal with.

She sat down once more and began rummaging through her large tote for something brightly colored to tie onto the hard-to-see fishing line. "Anyway, we need a new source of heat and energy. If one were out there, in the hands of the right people, I'd use it, and I'd be the first one to show others how to use it as well. I could revolutionize the world!"

Just then, a loud "Yeeoooowwww!" sounded across the deck. The umbrella rocked wildly. Angie spun around, realizing someone must have tripped over the line she'd just rigged up.

Dudley Livingstone. With his plump body and white clothes, and his arms waving helplessly, he looked like a tipsy Pillsbury Dough Boy. He caught himself against a table before he fell, which was good. If a man of his girth had landed on the deck, it wouldn't have been a pretty sight—for him or the deck.

But even more surprising than Livingstone's tripping over the wire was the fact that, when Angie looked up to see what was going on, she discovered that not only had Dudley Livingstone been close enough to hear every word she'd been saying, but so had all the other passengers, and Julio as well.

Why were all of them interested in what she had to say?

She caught Paavo's eye. Surely, this struck him as odd.

The Hydra moved back into the shadows. She'd noticed the passengers moving closer as Angie

Amalfi spoke, and had worked her way nearer as well. A new source of heat and energy? So she *did* know. Now the question was, had Sven been working with her from the start?

She should have known better than to trust the Norwegian with something this important. She was going to have to remedy it fast. Dămn! She couldn't afford any more mistakes. Too much was riding on this plan—it had to work, and work well.

If anyone else caused her trouble, they were dead.

11

"I need to make sure she does not try to pull a fast one on me." Colonel Ortega filled his beer glass with another Corona. He'd already drunk two six-packs during the afternoon, and now that dinner was over, he was starting on his third. If Eduardo Catalán had ever bothered to wonder where the man's huge gut came from, one day with him would have answered the question.

"She would not dare. Everyone knows your reputation." Catalán had a demitasse of black espresso on the lamp table at his elbow. They sat in the living room watching the sun sink behind the coast range to the west, Catalán on an easy chair, the colonel slouched down on the sofa, his head on the backrest and his feet up on the coffee table.

Ortega's dark eyes searched his. "I guess you are right."

"You worry too much, my colonel," Catalán said. "That is my job."

Ortega wouldn't drop it. "She would not have the reputation for reliability if she went around stealing from the men who employed her," he said, as much to himself as to Catalán.

"Exactly," Catalán said.

"But then, how many times has she had her hands on something worth millions? Something that every government, every industry in the world would want to possess? If she recognizes the true value of what she has, she will not want to release it for a mere million dollars." Ortega sat up straight, running his hands through his already messy hair. His clothes, in which he'd taken a siesta earlier that afternoon, were wrinkled and dirty.

"Especially when she learns you do not have the million to give her," Eduardo added.

Ortega's eyes narrowed. "Are you accusing me of being unfair, *amigo*?"

"Not unfair," Eduardo said, quick to correct himself. "Clever."

"Good." The colonel drank half a glassful before he put the beer down and wiped his mouth with the back of his hand. "I am always fair. She just has to wait a short time while I get the money. And the money will be twenty times—twenty, hell—*fifty* times over what I owe her, once I sell the formula to OPEC or whoever in the hell wants to pay me the most for it. Who knows, I might even be a real nice guy and sell it to Shell Oil in the U.S." He chuckled at the thought that he would soon actually possess something that every major world player in oil and gas would want to get their hands on.

"OPEC?" Catalán said. "You are not thinking of going over the heads of your friends, are you? Of cutting them out of the deal?"

Ortega shrugged. "What are friends for?" he said, then laughed. "Anyway, they would do the same to me if they had the opportunity."

Catalán nodded. "So you will work with whomever, and let the Hydra wait? Is that it?"

"She can wait. Or she can die. It is all up to her."

"You are clever indeed, my colonel."

12

At dinner that evening, Dudley Livingstone joined the other passengers and officers. He was seated on one side of Angie, Paavo on the other.

"How are you feeling after your near miss on the deck, Mr. Livingstone?" she asked. "I'm sorry I caused you to trip."

"No harm done," he said with a chuckle.

The Neblers and Cockburns were busy arguing over the merits of bridge versus canasta, Captain Olafson was quietly drinking, and Paavo was talking to Mr. Johansen about navigation. She wondered if he was more serious than she'd suspected about a job at sea.

"So tell me about your business, Mr. Livingstone," she said, feeling bad about ignoring the man at her side while the meal of Caesar salad, roast pork, mashed potatoes, and zucchini was being served.

He pressed a napkin to his lips, then folded his pudgy fingers before responding. "I'm basically an art dealer, Miss Amalfi. A dealer in South American antiquities. Right now, I'm escorting an Incan artifact back to Peru. It was found in Machu Picchu early in this century. It never should have been allowed to leave the country. It's priceless, you see, and the Peruvian government is paying quite handsomely for its return. It's in a container on this very ship. That's why I'm here: to ensure it arrives safely. Once in Peru, I'll see what I can find to take back to the States that can be legitimately sold to some very serious collectors or even museums there."

"So you buy and sell the things you find, for the most part?" she asked.

"To tell the truth, I only sell what I must in order to eat." He poured them each more white wine. "Mine is a very small, exclusive circle, Miss Amalfi," he continued. "I doubt anyone outside of it has ever heard of me. It's not as if many people want a ten-foot-tall Viracocha, the main Incan deity, sitting in their living room."

"No, I guess not," Angie admitted. "So, I take it you travel by freighter with your artifacts?"

"When time permits. I hate letting something priceless out of my hands for all the weeks it takes for shipment. Too much can happen to it."

"Oh?" Whatever could he do to save a container with a ten-foot statue even if something did happen to it? "Like what?"

He was clearly taken aback by her question, and his response did not answer it. "Well, to be frank, I enjoy this kind of travel. One meets interesting people. Tell me about yourself, Miss Amalfi."

"There's not much to tell. Currently, I'm a restaurant reviewer."

"Really? You must know a lot about cooking, I take it."

"A bit," she said, trying to sound modest.

"What kind?"

"All kinds." That, she had to admit, was less modest. "My specialties are French and Italian. I studied in Paris for a while."

"So you must know all kinds of tricks of the trade, such as how to enhance the flavor of fresh truffles, perhaps?"

"Is this a test, Monsieur Livingstone?"

"*Oui, mademoiselle.*" He looked so serious all of a sudden it made her uneasy.

"Are you talking about adding a little Madeira to the truffles?" she asked, although she was quite sure of the answer. "If so, I'd suggest doing that only to canned truffles—or should I say *truffes?*—which are a mere shadow of the fresh ones dug up from early December through the end of January. Nothing should be done to change one iota of the flavor of fresh *truffes*. Do I pass your test, *monsieur?*"

"With flying colors, *mademoiselle*. And now I must be off. Oh, one last thing. You didn't tell me about Mr. Smith. What line of work is he in?"

"Paavo is a San Francisco homicide inspector."

Suddenly, Angie noticed that the table grew absolutely silent. She turned from Livingstone, who had had all her attention. Quickly, the Neblars and Cockburns went back to their discussion. Had they been listening to her?

Then she remembered how they had all gathered close as she told Paavo about her idea for a cookbook. She began to eye them suspiciously.

"That's most interesting, Miss Amalfi," Livingstone said. She realized he was still talking about Paavo's job. He gulped down the wine.

Angie glanced at Paavo, but he continued talking with Johansen. He seemed to be the only one who hadn't noticed what had just ensued about his profession.

Just then, pecan pie was served for dessert, and once again, all conversation stopped.

13

After dinner, Angie and Paavo returned to their cabin. Angie went into the bedroom and changed to mauve silk lounging pajamas, purchased especially for this trip. When she returned to the sitting area, she found Paavo on the sofa with a book on his lap. He wasn't reading it, though. He was staring off into space. She'd seen that brooding look before. He noticed her and gave a faint smile.

She glanced at the one lamp on the end table beside the sofa.

Well, no wonder he wasn't reading. The lamp was so small, and the light bulb in it so weak, he'd get eyestrain in no time at all. Last night, sitting there and looking at a magazine, she had scarcely been able to see it. That, at least, was a problem she could solve.

She picked up the telephone. "Who are you calling?" Paavo asked, jarred from his reverie.

"You'll see," she said, giving him a smile and a wink. "Julio? This is Angie Amalfi. Do you have any larger lamps on board? I'd like to replace the one by the couch. I want a taller lamp with a brighter, stronger bulb." She waited. "Great. Thanks."

Paavo was surprised. "They actually have extra lamps on a freighter?"

"He'll probably swap this one with someone who doesn't care. It's no big deal."

Before long, there was a knock at the door. *"Buenos días, señorita."* Breathless, as if he'd run the whole way, Julio stood in the doorway holding a lamp so tall it could have served as a portable lighthouse. Angie gaped at it.

Julio gaped at her in her silk pajamas.

Paavo got up from the sofa and announced a sudden desire to change his shoes. He fled into the bedroom. Coward, Angie thought.

Julio entered the cabin, then handed Angie the big lamp and unplugged the little one on the end table. When he lifted it, one small button-like object fell off the base.

"What in the world?" Angie pointed at the floor. "The lamp is falling apart."

"What?" Julio stepped to the side, and she heard a crunch.

"Watch out!" she said, too late.

"I'm sorry," he cried. "Forgive me, *señorita.*" He dropped to the ground and started picking up the tiny pieces. "I didn't mean to break your whatever-it-is. I will replace it."

"It isn't mine. It's part of the lamp."

"I don't think so." He put the pieces in his pocket. "But it was not yours. That is good." Leaving the small lamp on the floor, he took the tall one from Angie, put it on the table, plugged it in, then switched it on. It didn't light. He switched light bulbs with the small lamp, and it still wouldn't light.

"What is wrong? There is . . . *nada*." He took off the bulb and studied the socket. Before Angie could say anything, he stuck his finger in the socket to prod it. Then, with a yelp, he jerked it out.

The electric current wasn't the problem.

"Are you all right?" Angie asked.

"*Sí, señorita.*" He sounded a little uncertain.

"Let's forget about the lamp. This new one is too big anyway. The smaller one will be fine."

"I will keep searching. Anything for you, *señorita.*" He put the small lamp back on the table and plugged it in.

"Thank you, Julio. Here you go." She handed him back the huge lamp.

He didn't turn around, though. Instead, he started backing out of the room, a toothy smile on his face, his longing gaze on her the whole time. At the door, he turned too quickly and crashed the lamp into the door frame. Blushing fiercely, he whispered, "*Adiós, señorita.*"

"*Adiós,* Julio," Angie said, then folded her arms and glared at the offending, still-remaining, too-small lamp.

"Is that walking destruction derby coming back soon?" Paavo called from the bedroom.

"He's just trying to be helpful," she said, joining him. "Although I must admit, he might be more helpful if he were less trying." She sighed.

"What was it that fell off the lamp?" Paavo asked.

"It was a little round disk."

"A disk?"

"That's right." Suddenly, her eyes opened wide and she spun toward him. "When Julio stepped on it, it broke open and had tiny wires. Paavo, it looked like a bug!"

His mouth wrinkled. "A bug?"

"A listening device, not an insect! What if our room was bugged?" She flung her arms in the air. "First someone goes through our bathroom cabinet, then they bug our lamp! What's with this place?"

He held his hands up, palms outward. "Angie, calm down. Now, tell me, do you know about lamp parts and wiring?"

"Well, no. But so what? I—"

"It was probably just a normal piece of the lamp."

"Let's find Julio and get it back. Then you can look at it and see for yourself."

"Not now. I think I'll read after all." He picked up his book.

"But Paavo—"

Obstinately, he shook his head. "You're letting your imagination run away with you, Angie.

Relax. Enjoy the cruise. Nothing is going on."

"How can you say that? Didn't you notice how whenever I ask about Sven or the cook, people change the conversation?" she asked.

"I think you were the one who was changing the conversation," he said.

"Me?"

"Come over here."

She crossed to his side. He took her hand and let his grip tighten, unable to hide the need he felt for her. He drew her onto the bed and she snuggled against him, the scent of her new perfume—a mixture of lilac and lilies—wafting over him. He kissed her, lightly at first, then deeply as his thoughts of how important she was to him enveloped him once more.

"I don't think—"

"You're changing the conversation again." As he pulled her down among the pillows, she wrapped her arms around him, returning his kisses as fast as he gave them.

"You taste so good," she whispered then smiled impishly. "Maybe this is the *Good Ship Lollipop*." She licked his ear.

He felt as if fireworks exploded all around him. "As long as it's not the *Titanic*."

Someone knocked on the door.

"It *is* the *Titanic*," Paavo groaned, flopping onto his stomach.

"Forget it," she said, running her hands over his shoulders.

The knock sounded again.

"If you don't go see who it is, you'll be wondering about it all night." He pulled the pillow over his head.

She was already off the bed. "It can't be anything serious." She walked to the door and opened it. To her amazement two men, one tall and the other short, stood in the dark hallway.

"Angie Amalfi?" the tall one asked.

"Yes," she replied.

"We heard you're a restaurant reviewer," the short one said.

"Why, yes." She'd heard of calling on doctors late at night, but never restaurant reviewers.

"We're the cooks," the taller one said. "Mike Jones here."

Mike Jones—what a simple name, she thought. Jones was a tall, slim, sandy-haired man, disarmingly handsome, wearing jeans and a blue pullover. He held out his hand. She took it and he gave her a strong, enthusiastic handshake, more like someone trying to sell Amway products than a cook.

"Andrew Brown," the short one said. "But I'm only Mike's assistant." He was young, short, and slender, with black hair and a peaked, almost washed-out look about his eyes. He, too, held out his hand in a firm handshake.

"You're both American," Angie said, unable to hide her surprise.

"That's because most of the passengers are," Jones explained. "We cook simple meals, but we'd like to cook something more. Pete Lichty was the experienced cook, a Dane, but since he's gone now—"

"That's why we came to see you," Brown added.

Did they expect her to cook? "Oh, well, I don't—"

"This is our free time—we don't have to cook for anyone at night—and we were wondering if you'd join us for a drink in the lounge." Jones smiled at her. A deep dimple marked his right cheek and its crease worked its way to his jaw. Young Andrew Brown seemed more washed out than ever by comparison.

Before she had a chance to reply, he quickly added, "We'd really enjoy talking to someone who knows good food and good cooking."

"Well . . ." She glanced over her shoulder. "One second."

Something told her not to call out Paavo's name as she walked back into the bedroom, and sure enough, his even breathing confirmed what she'd suspected might have happened— lying on the bed, he'd fallen asleep. Most likely, he'd be out for the night. He was still catching up on much-needed sleep. She hoped he'd catch up soon and again be the curious inspector she knew and loved.

Wait . . . where had that thought come from? He was giving up all that dangerous curiosity, and she was glad of it. She had to keep in mind the old saying about curiosity and the cat, and be glad of Paavo's new-found acquiescence.

She glanced at her watch. It was only nine o'clock. Heck, she might as well go to the lounge with Mike and Andrew. She certainly wasn't ready for bed. The only ones on board who were in bed this early were probably the Neblers, the Cockburns . . . and Paavo. She grabbed her tote bag.

"Let's go," she said, pulling the door quietly shut as she stepped into the hall.

They went down to the second deck, to the passenger lounge. In the ship's brochure, the room had been referred to as the "Panorama Lounge," even though there was nothing in the least panoramic about it. It had Formica tables, padded chairs, and large windows facing the sundeck, where the pool was found. Mike sent Andrew down to the galley, which was located below the main deck, to get some cold beers from the refrigerator.

Mike found a table in a dark corner of the room where, he said, they could sit and not be disturbed by anyone. Angie wasn't sure who might disturb them, since the other passengers had apparently gone to bed and the room was empty. As they made small talk about the chilly weather, Brown returned and put three cans of Budweiser on the table, without glasses. "We don't have anything fancy on a ship like this," he said. "Sorry."

"It's okay." Angie popped the top.

"So," Jones said, sitting back after drinking some of the beer, "tell us about cooking beef

Wellington. Just how do you get the meat to cook inside a pastry shell without burning the pastry to a crisp in the process?"

Angie was amazed at the question. That wasn't the sort of cooking tip she would have expected from beer-drinking freighter cooks. But if that was what they wanted to know . . .

Despite Angie's curiosity about how two such nice-looking young men had ended up working on a freighter, they had kept her talking almost nonstop, not only about beef Wellington, but about how to get the greatest height possible in a soufflé. How to make a dependable white sauce that could be counted on to work every time. How to apply the glaze to crème brulée.

"Enough already," she said with a laugh. "You're giving me a headache!"

"We're sorry," Jones said. "When we found out about your background, well . . ."

"Tell me about yourselves," Angie said. She turned to Andrew Brown. "You look very young to be working on a ship like this."

"I guess I am," Brown said, then glanced shyly at Jones and bowed his head. "I only got the job because of Mike."

"He needed work," Jones said matter-of-factly. "When I met him, he was eating out of the Dumpsters behind restaurants so that he wouldn't get sent to another foster home. He was willing to learn, and I needed an assistant who spoke English. I got tired of trying to communicate in anything from Norwegian to Chinese on these freighters. Not many Americans are involved in shipping anymore. So I told Captain Olafson we were a package deal—an inexpensive package deal. He took us on."

Angie faced Andrew. "So, is Mike treating you well?"

He gave a half smile. "Yeah, he's okay."

"And I take it," Angie continued, with sudden insight on how the young man would have had to escape the courts and child protective services, "Andrew Brown isn't your real name?"

Even in the dark corner, Angie could see Brown's eyes meet Jones's a moment before he looked down at the tabletop. "You could say that."

Angie smiled smugly as she turned back to Jones. "And you, Mr. Jones, how did you get started in this line of work?"

He grimaced. "I guess it was because of a woman. My ex-wife. After the divorce, I was cleaned out. I couldn't even get back on my feet because of alimony and child support payments—and they weren't even my kids. So I joined the ranks of deadbeat dads, or in my case, deadbeat cuckolded spouses responsible for other men's kids."

"Whoa, talk about a bitter speech," Angie said, surprised at the man's vehemence.

"Talk about a bitter man," he replied. "Say, Andy, maybe we should have another round of beer."

"Sure," she said. "And then you two can tell me about something I've been curious about since I got on this ship."

"Oh? What's that, Miss Amalfi?" Jones asked.

"Why the cook went running off. He seemed so anxious to get away, he even tried to jump! Working in the galley can't be that bad, can it?"

"He was always a comedian," Jones said. "It was just a joke. He'd planned to leave for some time."

"I hardly knew him," Andrew Brown said as he stood up. "Excuse me. I have to get up at four-thirty. The crew is served breakfast at six, well before the passengers eat."

"My goodness," Angie said. "I didn't realize that."

"You're right, Andy. I'd better come along, too." Jones stood as well. "Good night, Miss Amalfi, and thank you for all your help."

With that, they both left.

Angie stared after them. Was it something she'd said?

14

He saw the small white house again. He was standing beside Yosh, and it was too quiet. He should have said something. The quiet bothered him. Something was wrong. He opened his mouth, trying to speak, to warn them. But no sound came out. He tried to yell, but he couldn't. No matter how hard he tried to tell them to get back, he couldn't speak, couldn't cry out.

He opened his eyes but still couldn't shake the vision of the house in the distance, and directly in front of him, the shoulders of men in dark blue, easing closer, closer to the house, just as they'd planned.

Then the blast.

And red . . . red oozing against the dark blue.

He felt again the hands that pushed him back, out of the way, out of the line of fire.

Paavo sat up. His heart was pounding from the dream, from the memory of the shoot-out, of Ed Gillespie being hit. He looked down at his arms, his hands. But the blood that had sprayed all over him when Ed was shot was gone now.

He stood and ran his hands over his eyes, through his hair.

Today the city would be holding a funeral for Sergeant Ed Gillespie. A police officer's funeral. Grand, poignant, and unbearably sad.

He walked out into the sitting area and sat down on the sofa as the scene replayed yet again, as vividly as the day it happened.

Hours passed. As the sun rose, Paavo felt the ship's engines begin to vibrate. He went to the window and watched as they slowly left Long Beach harbor.

He wasn't sure how long he stood there before the creaking of the bed told him Angie had awakened. Quickly he sat down and opened a book.

"Good morning," she said sleepily, stumbling into the sitting area.

"Good morning to you, too." He held out his hand. She walked over and placed hers in his and he pulled her down beside him on the sofa. Her hand tightened and she smiled, then yawned.

"Did you sleep well?" he asked, lightly touching her face, her cheek.

"Quite well. What about you? Have you been up long?"

"Since five or so," he said, putting his arm around her back and drawing her head to his shoulder. She felt warm and cuddly. "I fell asleep early."

"So I noticed. Still, that's much too early to get up," she declared, running her hand over his chest, his stomach. His nose pressed against her hair, and he breathed in her warm, musky scent. He could feel his body come alive, his nerves tingling, taut.

"Maybe you need to go back to bed and start the day all over again," she added.

"You may be right," he whispered. Just then, his gaze caught his watch—eight-thirty. Ed's funeral would start at nine.

He suddenly felt cold and all but dead inside. His gaze met Angie's for a moment, then he turned his head away and shut his eyes. *Damn!*

He stood. "I think I'll go try to find out how Sven Ingerson is doing. I'll be back soon." He forced a smile. "It's day three of our vacation, after all. Time to get up and enjoy it."

15

Angie sat on the sofa after Paavo walked out the door.

She wasn't sure what to do. On the one hand, everything he said and did was in keeping with a man on vacation, a man who didn't want other people's troubles, issues, and strange behavior to interfere with his life.

In other words, he wasn't acting like a cop. Terrific. Wasn't that exactly what she wanted? She'd always thought that was what she wanted. But now that she had it, she couldn't say for sure that the new Paavo pleased her—especially when there was something strange happening on this ship. Not anything very serious, she supposed, but something, nonetheless.

More than once her belongings had been handled, moved around a bit. Or so it had seemed. It couldn't be her imagination, could it?

Everything should be fine once they reached Acapulco and the beautiful villa she'd arranged for them to use while there.

One of her father's friends owned an ocean-side estate just a little south of Acapulco, and rarely used it. So she'd told her father all about her "Dining Out in Acapulco" magazine assignment, and then asked if he thought the villa might be available for a few days.

"Stay a week, Angelina," Sal had said. "A month. Longer if you want. There are lots of restaurants in Acapulco, you know."

Angie knew his motive. He wanted her far away from Paavo. Sal didn't like the idea of his youngest daughter falling in love with a cop and hoped she would get over it quickly. He seemed to think a doctor or a lawyer—even a politician—would be a better choice for a husband. He'd find a way to free up the villa if he had to buy it himself.

So she hadn't told him Paavo would be joining her.

Sal got her the villa.

But thoughts of Acapulco weren't helping her here and now. Suddenly a solution came to mind. Even if Paavo wouldn't listen to her, Captain Olafson would.

She quickly dressed and ran up to the pilot house to talk to him.

First Mate Johansen was standing on the bridge, staring out at sea. He turned at her approach.

"Excuse me," she said. "I was looking for Captain Olafson."

"I'm sorry," he replied. "The captain is indisposed. May I help you?" He showed Angie into his office and left the door open.

She sat in the chair he indicated, and studied him as she tried to come up with a way to begin. "I came to alert you to something strange. A bug may have been placed in my room. A listening device, not an insect."

"A *bug*?" Angie had the distinct feeling Johansen thought she was crazy. She was getting that reaction far too often to suit her. "May I see it?" he asked.

"Your steward, Julio, took it away."

"I'll ask him if he can retrieve it, then we can both determine exactly what it was." Johansen stood. "I'm sorry if our accommodations are not what you expected, Miss Amalfi. We'll do what we can to make the rest of your journey more pleasant."

Angie also stood. "By the way, how is Mr. Ingerson doing?

"Sven Ingerson?" Johansen's eyebrows rose in surprise. "I didn't think a case of food poisoning would interest the passengers. We think that's all that's wrong with him. He was taken to the hospital. The paramedics took all the particulars about his home address and the company representatives that they should contact. Unfortunately, it isn't unheard of for seamen to get sick or hurt and have to go to hospitals on shore. We have no sick bay on board, only first aid. It's not as if the ship can wait for them to get better. We just sail on and do the best we can. I hope this doesn't seem too unfeeling to you."

"Well, I suppose I understand your reasons." There was nothing more to be said. "Thank you for your time."

"Have a pleasant voyage, Miss Amalfi," Johansen said, almost as an afterthought.

"I'd like to speak to one of your patients, Sven Ingerson, please," the Hydra said into the telephone.

"Ingerson . . . Ingerson," the hospital receptionist repeated softly. "Oh, here he is. I'm sorry. He's in intensive care and unable to take calls."

"It's very important. A matter of life and death. I must speak with him immediately."

"Let me put you through to the nurse in charge."

She drummed her fingers, waiting for the transfer to be made. The phone rang.

"ICU. Nurse Patel."

"This is Dagmar Ingerson—Sven Ingerson's sister. I'd like to speak with him, please."

"I'm sorry, but he isn't able to speak at the moment. Have you talked to his doctor?"

"Not yet. I really just need one moment with Sven. It's an emergency. I won't disturb him again after this, I promise."

"I'm sorry. You must speak with the doctor."

"Please, Nurse," she tried to make her voice
tearful. "Ten seconds. I'm really desperate."

"I'd help you if I could, but your brother . . .
he's very serious. Critical, I'm afraid. He
wouldn't be physically able to speak with you
even if it were permitted."

16

That night, Angie approached the bed wearing the beautiful negligee she'd bought especially for this romantic vacation. Some romance! Paavo had been distant all day, smiling and pleasant—and completely out of character. He'd even teamed up as Ruby Cockburn's partner in a game of bridge.

The sea had grown rougher throughout the evening, so bad that the captain ordered cold sandwiches for dinner. He didn't want any cooking going on in the galley, or any chance of hot food being spilled on anyone's lap. Now, the ship's rolling made her lurch awkwardly from side to side. She wanted to swing her hips, not her whole body.

Paavo was sitting up in bed waiting for her, a blanket covering him from the waist down. The area below his left shoulder held only a faint shadow of the scar from the gunshot that had nearly killed him soon after they first met. She proudly remembered how she had stopped the gunman from firing a second shot as Paavo lay wounded . . . and she'd been in love with him ever since.

Standing by the doorway, she slowly removed her dressing gown, revealing a negligee of silk and lace, antique gold in color, that fell unfettered from her shoulders to the floor. By the time the gown dropped, Paavo's large blue eyes burned with desire. In that area, at least, he was still the man she knew and loved. She walked toward him, step by step, trying not to stumble, and reminding herself of how beautifully the material glimmered as she moved. He seemed to hold his breath.

When she reached him, he took her hands in his. "You're beautiful, Angie. I could spend hours doing nothing but look at you."

"Sorry," she whispered, then bent forward and kissed him. "Not good enough."

Angie was dreaming she was on a roller-coaster ride. On the roller coaster with her was Sven Ingerson, Dudley Livingstone, Julio Rodriguez, and the mysterious cook who'd tried to jump off the ship when she first arrived. She should have followed his example.

She woke up to find the dream was scarcely an exaggeration. The storm was making a terrible racket; rain and waves pounded the ship and the wind howled. Crushed between the high padded edge of the bed and Paavo, she had to practically fight her way to a sitting position. The fact that he didn't wake up indicated just how tired he still was. She couldn't help but wonder if this constant fatigue didn't have something to do with his decision to quit his job—not that he was physically ill, because he seemed otherwise healthy, but simply because it was weighing on his mind.

God, but she felt sick. She clutched the side of the bed, hanging over the edge. She had no idea such a huge ship could bounce around this way. She imagined it looking like a toy boat in a bathtub with a little kid smacking the water.

She groaned, her stomach feeling queasier with each roll of the boat way, way up, then way, way down.

Maybe some water would help. She reached for her negligee at the foot of the bed, slipped it on, then, holding onto the furniture, lurched her way into the bathroom.

She took a sip of water, then turned to go back to bed. Just then a stronger roll of the ship sent her reeling across the bathroom floor. As she stumbled past the medicine cabinet, she caught sight of her deathly pale face in the mirror.

She clutched her rapidly worsening stomach. She needed to go back to bed and lie down immediately. On the other hand, she didn't think it would be a good idea to get too far away from the bathroom.

She worked her way back toward the bedroom and looked at Paavo. He was now stretched across the bed catty-corner, still sleeping soundly.

Then she remembered the wall bed. At least there she could lie down and be near the bathroom—which, her stomach told her, was becoming increasingly necessary with every roll of the ship.

Bracing herself, she lunged toward the wall bed, flipped up the two metal clamps that held the lengthwise bed against the wall, and tugged on it, lowering the bed all the way down. Then she hurled herself on top of it, clutching the thin mattress so she wouldn't fall off. Just lying down on her stomach that way helped her feel a lot better. She spread her arms so that her hands gripped the edges of the narrow mattress.

As the ship tossed about, the bow of the ship dipped. Her feet went up, her head down. She hadn't been this far upside down since she tried taking a yoga class and had to stand on her head. Then the ship crested and her head rose high in the air, pointing toward heaven, her feet toward the other place. She felt like a little kid playing airplane. She'd heard that tropical storms were furious but short, and prayed it was true. This one had gone on long enough already.

She tried to relax. She shut her eyes and willed herself back to sleep. Unfortunately, her thoughts were of past cruises she'd been on—ships with stabilizers, with tremendous varieties of gourmet food, with dancing, big swimming pools, even hot tubs. Her breathing deepened. Miniature golf, boutiques, a sauna. She let go of the mattress, turning on her side to go to sleep. A deluxe stateroom with a deep bath . . .

As she began to doze, one side of the ship rolled upward in a long, slow climb, higher and higher, and suddenly she felt herself slide right off the mattress and against the wall. And still the boat climbed. She couldn't even think of being seasick now, certain the ship would flip over and they'd be upside down in the water. She really didn't want to be here any longer.

The far side of the ship began to lower itself and she began to breathe again, although still tucked against the wall. But then, once more, it began to rise.

The edge of the bed rose higher and higher.

Suddenly, the bed itself, free now of her weight spread full on it to hold it down, suddenly bounded upward, right off the floor, and swung up into the wall, squashing her against it like a fly.

The Hydra dialed the familiar number. "It's me."

"You!"

She smiled at the sound of fear in the man's voice. It was exactly what she wanted to hear. That meant she could take care of this matter quickly, then go to the galley and do another quick search of a few things. "Listen, the *Valhalla* is supposed to dock in Cabo San Lucas tomorrow. I don't want it to."

"What's up?"

"There are some people on board who I don't want getting off the ship. They've got something of mine, and no one is leaving this crate until it's in my hands. You've got to help."

"Hey, I can't perform miracles."

"I don't want a miracle, just a bribe. I don't care who you get to—the harbormaster, the head of the dockworkers, some politician, but whoever it is, they need to tell the captain that there's a strike going on and no one is available to load or unload his containers. Tell him that the people he sees working are scabs, and the union is ready to start gunplay if any more scabs are hired. The one doing the hiring might be the first to get shot. I know this captain. Believe me, he won't think twice about docking if he thinks there's any danger possible."

"A strike?"

"I don't care who you get to give him the news, but it had better be good."

"How much is it worth?"

"Ten thousand, max."

"Twenty."

"Fifteen."

"Eighteen."

"Seventeen."

"Done."

*   *   *

Angie pushed hard on the mattress, and as the ship rolled in the other direction, the mattress lowered with a whump.

She sat up on it. Her hair was standing on end—probably from the fury she felt. She would have been even more angry about this whole miserable trip except that she was too busy brushing dust off herself and running her hands over her face and arms and through her hair.

That had been one of the most horrible experiences of her life. Holding onto walls and furniture, she got off the wall bed—she had never thought they were called that because you could get walled up inside one—and went to tell Paavo all about it.

To her complete amazement, he was still asleep.

She put on her robe and slippers to go to the galley and find something to settle her stomach. She felt parched, seasick, and generally miserable. Being shoved into a wall by a mattress will do that to you.

17

Where was the galley? She'd been told it was just below the main deck, near the crew's mess, but she'd never been this far down in the ship before. She thought she was on the right deck, though. Maybe she should have taken the elevator instead of the stairs, but the elevator was so slow. She'd expected there would be a large sign on the door, something like the kitchen sign in a big hotel.

There seemed to be nothing but closed doors down here. The galley wouldn't have regular doors. They'd be swinging ones—or so she hoped. Things weren't that different on a freighter, or were they?

The decks below the main deck were larger than those that rose above it in the superstructure at the rear of the freighter. But even here, in the hull of the ship, most of the space was taken up by massive containers.

She turned a corner and saw two large doors up ahead. It had to be the galley—with double doors large enough to roll carts of food out to the mess and up the elevator to the passenger's dining room. She walked up to it and pushed the door open.

A flashlight blinded her, then went off. Startled, she froze momentarily, then turned to run when a hand grabbed her wrist and yanked her into the dark galley. "No!" she screamed as she was flung into the room.

She stumbled forward, banging into a rack of pots and pans. They fell over with a loud clatter, and so did she.

She lay without moving. The only sound she heard was the swishing of the galley door back and forth until it stilled.

Was she alone? She waited, scarcely breathing, listening for any sound that might tell her that her assailant was still in the room.

Nothing except the heavy pounding of her heart.

She inched her way toward the door and was ready to run out when she heard a *plop-plop-plop* sound in the hallway. She scooted back to where she had been and found what she wanted—an enormous cast-iron frying pan.

Now that her eyes had grown used to the dark, she could see the narrow line of light from the hallway beneath the galley doors, so she knew where her assailant would be coming from. She carefully, quickly eased to the side of the door, the frying pan hoisted over her shoulders like a baseball bat.

The door was pulled open slowly, then stopped. From the dim night-light in the hallway a hand reached into the galley. She was sure she was going to faint.

A long gown floated against the door's opening. It was either a woman or a ghost, she thought. But there were no such things as ghosts, so it had to be a woman. Must be Nellie or Ruby. No problem. Although it seemed a little tall for Nellie . . . even for Ruby.

Maybe she should call out, greet them.

But what if she was wrong?

Something rubbed against the wall, up and down, up and down. Then it stopped. She gripped the frying pan tighter, raising it higher.

Suddenly the lights came on.

Angie screamed.

Julio screamed.

Julio?

Angie kept the frying pan raised, not sure if she could trust him or not. The steward stood before her wearing a long nightshirt and slippers with no backs, the kind that flopped when you walk in them.

"*Señorita,* you scared me!" he cried. "What are you doing here in the dark? In the middle of the night? With a frying pan?"

"Someone attacked me."

"*Madre mia!* Are you all right?"

She slowly lowered her arms. "Just a little

banged up. I came down here because I felt seasick," she said. "But someone was here ahead of
me. With a flashlight. Did you see anyone in the
hall?"

"No, *señorita,* no one at all."

"What are you doing here?"

"Me? I wanted some warm milk. I could not
sleep with so much trouble—first the cook leaving, then my friend Sven getting sick. I am trou-
bled."

"You're not the only one," she murmured.

"Where is Mr. Smith? Why are you here
alone?" he asked.

"Paavo's sleeping like a baby."

"Then please join me. I will have my warm
milk, and you can have your soda, and we will
wait out this storm together." He pointed at the
frying pan she still held. "I think you can put
that down now."

She eyed him suspiciously. "I'll put it down . . .
but I'll keep it in easy reach."

Paavo became aware, in a semiasleep state, that
the storm was much worse than anyone had
expected it would be. The best thing to do was
to try to sleep through it, to ignore the roar of
the sea, the banging of rain against the windows, the almost human cry of the wind
through the ship.

He reached out to Angie. She wasn't there.
She must have gotten up to use the bathroom.
Maybe her getting up was what had awakened

him. He rolled over to go back to sleep.

When he awoke again, the sun was peeking over the horizon. He turned over to check on Angie, but she still wasn't beside him. Was she up already? That wasn't like her. He remembered a terrible storm last night. He sat up, suddenly wide awake. Where was Angie?

He got out of bed and hurried to the sitting area. Empty. The bathroom door was open. Empty.

The wall bed was down. What was that supposed to mean? Had she tried sleeping on it? Had she grown so out of sorts with him that she didn't want to sleep with him anymore? Things had seemed okay between them last night. He remembered her talking . . . she was talking about writing a cookbook again . . . and he remembered getting more and more sleepy . . . he must have . . . oh, hell.

Christ, where was she? His heart began to race. He couldn't see her leaving the cabin on her own. She never got up this early on vacation. She never got up early, period. A cold, ugly dread seeped through him. He was ready to run out, then realized he was in his pajamas. He needed to put on his shoes and pants at least. God, what if she'd been hurt? She'd been curious about this ship, about the strangeness going on here, but he'd dismissed it, ignored the danger. That was what civilians did, he'd supposed: ignore danger, then rush headlong into it.

He tore off his pajamas. Before leaving the

city, he'd decided he was through with police work, through investigating, through having to deal with all the grief caused by men who went bad.

Yet, early in the cruise he'd begun to develop an uneasy feeling about this ship. Like Angie, he'd noticed that things had been moved around their room as if it had been searched; he'd noticed Livingstone's strange questions, Sven Ingerson's strange words and illness, even the way everyone seemed to be constantly watching Angie. Most of those things were explainable and clearly meant nothing ominous. But not all of them were.

He put on underwear and his jeans. The damnable part was that he hadn't allowed himself to differentiate the serious from the trivial. He'd chosen to ignore them all instead of trying to find out what the hell was really going on here. And now he didn't know where Angie was.

He pulled a sweater over his head. In a flash, his mind filled with all the horrible possibilities of what could happen to a young woman on a ship like this, in the middle of the ocean. That was the trouble with having been a homicide inspector. He'd seen people's worst nightmares come true.

She had to be all right. He had to find her.

His head pounded with the effort of pushing away his grisly thoughts. Where were his shoes? Everything was topsy-turvy in the cabin. He was ready to tear something apart—

Just then the door opened. Angie came waltz-
ing into the room, and when she saw him, she
smiled. "Well, look who's awake," she said cheer-
ily. "Good morning."

He stared at her. That was all? Just good
morning? She was still wearing her night things,
her robe. She looked happy, dammit, while he'd
just aged ten years. "Where the hell were you?"

She arched an eyebrow. "I couldn't sleep. I
was with Julio. And I've got so much to tell you!"

Had he heard right? "Julio! At this time of
night?"

Her eyes narrowed ominously. "It's morning
now. Anyway, I wanted some 7-Up to settle my
stomach, and—"

He stepped closer, suddenly furious. "You
called him in the middle of the night?"

She gaped at him, acting shocked that he was
talking to her in that tone. Well, what did she
expect after what she'd done? "I didn't call anyone! I went to the galley."

"How innocent. And he just happened to be
waiting?" Even he hated the way he sounded,
but for the life of him he couldn't stop himself.
"I suppose he offered comfort. And you took it!"

Her cheeks flamed. "Thank goodness he was
there," she yelled. "All things considered!"

So she *was* glad! She *did* like the man!
"What's that supposed to mean?"

Angie lifted her chin, clearly every bit as
angry as he was. "We sat in the galley and talked.
Julio is a nice man. Very nice, in fact. He's plan-

ning on going back to school and becoming a geography teacher. This is his field research."

"Sure it is." At least the weaselly twerp hadn't said he needed field research to become a gynecologist.

"Don't be snippy."

She took off her robe and tossed it across a chair. The nightgown looked as thin and beautiful at dawn as it had last night. He remembered how it felt in his hands, how she felt in his hands. He wondered if Julio had caught a glimpse of it.

He stepped closer to her. "Don't you know better than to traipse around like that?" he shouted.

She folded her arms. "You are clearly in no mood to listen to a word I have to say."

"I *am* listening. But so far, I haven't heard anything worth listening to!"

"You are unbelievable!" she cried, flinging out her arms in fury. "And I didn't traipse anywhere. I was seasick."

He clenched his fists, imagining the steward's scrawny neck in them. "Well, Julio seemed to have taken care of your problem."

"He did." She spoke through gritted teeth. "Very nicely, thank you."

What did she mean by that? "You could have woken me up. I would have helped you."

"Excuse me. I'm going to bed. I need some sleep."

He watched her flounce away.

"Wait a minute. What are those bruises on your arm?"

She glanced over her shoulder at him. "I guess Julio likes to play rough."

She slammed the bedroom door shut.

18

Eduardo Catalán enjoyed watching the terrified expressions on the faces of the clerks in the harbor master's office when Colonel Hector Ortega himself marched up to the front desk. He had put his military jacket on over his wrinkled white shirt, the same one he had worn the day before. Now, standing before one of the clerks, his thick brows arrogantly lifted, he demanded to know when the *Valhalla* would arrive.

"The . . . the what?" were the most coherent words the unfortunate young woman could stammer.

"*Valhalla!* A freighter. A Norwegian freighter. It is coming from the United States. Do you not know about it?"

The woman's cheeks went from white to red. "We . . . we have many ships arriving here, *señor,* and many freighters, and—"

"I know that!" he roared. "I do not care about your many ships. I care about one ship. One!"

"Yes, *señor*—"

"Colonel!"

"I mean, Colonel." On the verge of tears, she picked up her schedule and ran to the back of the office for help.

"You see, my colonel," Catalán said, "why you must allow me to handle such annoyances for you. The people who are supposed to serve these days . . . they are so abysmal."

"I need to know right away, Eduardo," the colonel said as he turned his back to the clerks bustling about searching for the answer to his question, "exactly where she is."

"Colonel Ortega," the clerk called softly.

The colonel spun around. "You have the information." His words were a command, not a question.

She nodded timidly. "The *Valhalla* left Long Beach two days ago. It hasn't reached Cabo San Lucas yet. It's scheduled to be there two days, then head to Mazatlán after that."

"Long Beach? It was not scheduled to stop in Long Beach!" he bellowed.

"I am sorry, Colonel. That is my information." She backed up.

He spun around, his eyes bulging as he spat out his words to Eduardo. "Why does she not take a plane like everyone else in the world? Do something, *amigo,* to get that ship here sooner. I do not like to wait." Then he stormed from the building.

*   *   *

The American turned away from the rack of brochures he'd hovered over the entire time Colonel Ortega had been talking to the clerk. Ortega rarely moved from his mountain retreat. To see him in the city meant that something was happening. Something big.

And George Gresham knew he was the one to find out what it was all about.

Gresham took off the blue denim cap with fish lures on it—his tourist disguise—and ran his thick, square fingers through his blond crew cut, trying to ignore the ever-enlarging bald spot on the crown. As a field operative, he'd always kept his hair short. Now he kept it short thinking people might not realize that some of it was actually missing.

But he had no time for misplaced vanity. He had to keep an eye on Ortega. He was beside himself with joy that this little jaunt had paid off. It showed his instincts were as sharp as ever.

The *Valhalla*. Not only would the colonel be waiting for it, but George would be there, too. Especially to find out who the mysterious "she" was that Ortega talked about.

He couldn't wait to tell the others.

19

Angie went up to the bridge to watch the *Valhalla* sail into the small, colorful harbor of Cabo San Lucas. The other passengers already lined the rail.

When she had awakened in late morning, with a dull headache from her miserable sleep and aches all over her body from the way she'd fallen in the galley, Paavo was gone. She didn't know where. She was so steamed at him for assuming the worst that right now she couldn't say she cared.

The captain stepped out of the pilot house and called the passengers together. He looked considerably better this morning than he had the night before, actually sober for once. Johansen was nowhere to be seen.

"Quiet, please," he cried. "May I have your attention?"

The tiny band of passengers huddled

together waiting for him to speak couldn't have been any more quiet if they'd been dead.

"Ladies and gentlemen," he shouted. "I have bad news for you. The dockworkers at Cabo San Lucas have gone on strike. The strike is expected to last for a number of days. They have threatened me—I mean, our crew—with violence if we attempt to load or unload the containers ourselves. Therefore, we are not stopping until we reach Mazatlán. We'll try this port again on our return trip. I apologize for any inconvenience."

"Gracious," Nellie cried. "Do you think it's safe, Marvin?"

"Might turn ugly," Ruby said. "Might come on board. We could be captured. Raped."

"Oh, Lord!" Nellie pressed her hands to her chest.

"Not to worry," Marvy Marv muttered.

"What?" Harold asked, putting his hands to his ears.

"What will you do?" Angie asked Ruby. "Weren't you and Harold planning to leave the ship at Cabo?"

"Were. But we changed our minds. Can't find good bridge partners too often. We're staying with the Neblers. Tierra del Fuego or bust, that's our motto."

Angie was speechless. Borrowing the binoculars Marvy Marv wore around his neck, she studied the harbor. For a place with a dockworkers' strike going on, it looked surprisingly busy, and the piers bustled with longshoremen handling cargo.

Yet the *Valhalla* wasn't allowed to dock. It didn't make sense.

"Miss Amalfi?"

Angie was lying on a chaise longue by the pool with a light sunscreen on her face and suntan oil slicked over every inch of skin not covered by the skimpy teal-blue DKNY bikini. She opened her eyes at the sound of the silky voice calling her name. Mike Jones stood at her feet, a smile digging his dimple deeper than ever. "Good afternoon," she said.

He grabbed hold of a chair under an umbrella-covered table, spun the chair around backward, and sat down straddling it. "I wanted to ask a favor of you," he said.

"Sure. What can I do for you?"

"Since you know a lot about cooking," Jones began, "I was wondering if you could you guide me in the preparation of a really nice meal for tonight's dinner. I know the passengers are all upset about not being able to land, so I thought a good meal might make it up to them a bit—if you see what I mean."

"That's a very thoughtful suggestion," she admitted, wondering why she felt so amazed that it had come from Jones. "Tomorrow we'll arrive in Mazatlán, and everyone can disembark there, so you're quite right—getting through this evening will be the problem. If we give the passengers good food and some wine with the meal, they'll most likely feel a whole lot better about themselves and each other."

"I was hoping you'd see it that way. Andrew Brown will be there to assist as well—he does the chopping and lots of the tedious work."

"A sous-chef, of sorts."

"Whatever." He gave her a perplexed grin.

"I'll come by in about an hour, and we'll see what's available in your larder," Angie said.

He stood. "I appreciate it, Miss Amalfi. By the way . . . great swimsuit."

The emergency alert sent every free doctor and nurse in the intensive care unit running to help.

Wearing a resident's white coat with a stethoscope strung around his neck, a spiral-bound reference book jammed into his pocket, a satchel in one hand, a clipboard in the other, and a tired, glazed expression on his grimly determined face, a long-legged man continued resolutely down the hospital corridor.

Staring at him, a nurse frowned with confusion and hurried after him. He stopped at Sven Ingerson's room and lifted the medical chart from the rack on the door, then wearily glanced up at her.

"I need to check in on Mr., uh—" He scanned the page on the chart as he put it on his clipboard. "Ingerson."

"You do?"

"Did you need to see this patient now, nurse?"

"I don't believe so," she replied, wide-eyed and worried-looking.

As he glanced from the chart to her, his brow furrowed deeper. He put his hand on the door, ready to push it open and enter.

She took a step toward the room.

He froze. "Are you new here?" he asked sternly.

"Yes," she said hesitantly, easing back. "This is my first day in this unit."

He nodded briskly. The young nurse stood, alert but anxious as he opened the door a crack and peered at Ingerson.

The patient appeared to be asleep, masses of tubes stuck into his arms and nose.

He scanned the chart again. "Hmm."

"What is it, doctor?" the nurse asked.

"Shouldn't he be awake by now?"

"But . . . as you see in the chart, the botulism was too far advanced by the time we saw him. He's not expected to last the night. All we can do is keep him comfortable."

"Yes." He took off his stethoscope and lightly rapped it against his hand while staring at her. He ran a finger up and down the long, flexible cord. His gaze jumped from it, to her thin neck.

"There's an emergency under way," he said abruptly. "Don't you think you should check on the other patients while their nurses are busy trying to save a life? I don't need my hand held."

The young nurse blushed fiercely. "Oh, I'm

sorry. I didn't mean . . . excuse me, doctor." She hurried down the hall.

As soon as she was gone, he entered the room, shutting the door behind him. "Sven," he called, his hand on the patient's chest. "Sven, wake up! The Hydra sent me. The Hydra. Even if you're asleep, you've got to know what that means." He waited. "Come on, Sven! I can't give her no for an answer, and you know it."

He lifted Ingerson's eyelids. "Yo, Sven!" He shone a light into the glazed eyes, but Sven seemed to be somewhere over the rainbow.

He turned around and started to go through Ingerson's belongings—the clothes he'd been wearing and his papers—but quickly gave up and simply stuffed them all into his satchel. He walked over to Sven again. "Wake up, god-dammit. She's going to fry us both. I might as well crawl into the bed next to you right now, 'cause that's where I'll end up if you don't tell me where in the hell you put the microfilm, or whatever it is. She won't tell me what's on it, the bitch. What does she think, that I'll steal it from her or something? Goddammit, Sven." He grabbed Sven by the shoulders and started shaking him. "Wake the hell up!"

"Doctor?"

He looked up. The young nurse was standing in the doorway staring at him, her mouth gaping.

He withdrew his hands and stepped back. "It's the latest technique, nurse," he said. "The

brain, you see, actually does hear and understand what's going on, even if the patient
appears to be in a deep sleep or coma. So, you
just demand that he wake up. Sometimes it
works."

He grabbed his clipboard and headed out the
door. "And then sometimes it doesn't."

20

About an hour later, Angie changed to a simple yellow cotton dress and walked into the galley. Mike Jones and his assistant, Andrew Brown, were in a corner talking, Brown perched on a counter and Jones sitting in a chair. They smiled in greeting when they saw her, Brown quickly hopping off the counter and retreating to the back of the kitchen with his habitual timidity.

"Please make yourself at home, Miss Amalfi," Jones said, approaching her. "I leave it to you to look around and decide what you'd like to cook. We've got a pretty good selection of spices and foods to choose from."

"I will, thanks," Angie said.

"Can I take your things?" Jones asked as he led her to the food storage room.

All she had was her tote bag. "It's no problem," she said, putting it down just inside the door. She immediately began checking canned goods on shelves, refrigerated items, and those in an enormous freezer compartment. After last night's storm, she could understand why everything was so snugly packed and braced. If her kitchen at home had been thrown around the way this galley and storage area was, everything she owned would be in the middle of the floor in a thousand pieces.

She checked the meat and fish, telling herself it didn't matter that Paavo hadn't joined her out by the pool. It was clear he wasn't at all interested in how she would be spending the rest of the afternoon.

Had he joined her now, the only thing he could have done was peel garlic, anyway. He was great at it once she'd showed him the trick of slightly mashing the clove with the handle of the chopping knife to help separate the skin from the meat. He stirred well, too. But he'd be checking his watch every few minutes and wondering when she'd be finished. Good cooking was not something to be accomplished with a stopwatch.

All in all, she decided, she'd be better off without him underfoot. Besides, she was still trying to stay angry at him. Her and Julio? Honestly!

"Did the storm last night bother either of you very much?" she asked Jones and Brown, who stood by, mutely watching her.

"It was all I could do not to fall out of bed," Jones replied. "I was sick as a dog."

"It scared me," said the soft-spoken Brown, hovering behind her.

"How did you do?" Jones asked her.

Angie decided not to tell them about the wall bed incident. "It kept me awake," was all she offered.

She found some fish fillets. "Oh, Mike, are these fillets Pacific petrale sole, by any chance? Or are they plain old flounder?"

"I don't know," he said truthfully.

What kind of cook didn't know the type of fish in his own kitchen? These boys needed her help even more than she'd thought.

She went to the larder and began loading her arms with onion, garlic, and spices. "Let me help you with that," Jones said, running to her assistance. Brown shyly hung back, doing only what Jones asked him to.

Together, making several trips, they carried the vegetables, vermicelli, vinegar, butter, and potatoes, as Angie directed, into the work area of the galley. She noticed Jones pick up her tote bag and begin to walk toward the door with it.

"Where are you going with that?" she asked.

He spun around. "I was just going to . . . put it on the counter so that it doesn't get stepped on."

"You can leave it on the floor by the wall over there. It won't get hurt. I need all the counter space possible."

"Whatever you say." He flashed her one of his deep-dimpled smiles.

Ignoring him for the moment, Angie planned

her meal. She'd start with *soupe au pistou*, a
Provençal vegetable soup with carrots, leeks,
green beans, zucchini, tomato, and vermicelli,
flavored by the *pistou*, which was made by crushing basil and garlic with a mortar and pestle,
then adding Parmesan cheese and olive oil. Next
she'd serve a spinach salad with a vinaigrette
dressing. The main course would be poached
fish fillets in white wine with mushrooms, served
with parsley potatoes. For dessert, she decided
on a simple chocolate *pot de crème*. Due to the
ship's limited provisions, the ingredients of this
meal wouldn't be remarkable, but what she did
with them would be.

They needed to prepare the soup first, then
the *pot de crème* and the potatoes, and last of all,
just before time to serve, she would poach the
fish. All afternoon, with Jones's assistance and
Brown acting as silent backup in the pantry,
chopping and dicing, she worked on the meal.
Despite the time it took, she looked forward to
seeing the expressions on the passengers' faces
when they discovered what it was like to have a
meal by a real cook.

She suspected more than one of them
thought she was just blowing smoke when she'd
talked about being a restaurant reviewer and
knowing a bit about gourmet cooking.

There were times when she loved showing
off.

She was turning the flame under the potatoes
to a low boil when she heard a thud and saw

Mike Jones stumble. "Oops, just kicked your tote," he said. "We've really got to do something about it." He picked it up and handed it to Brown, who'd just emerged from the pantry. "I don't want anything to get crushed. You have sunglasses in it, don't you?"

"Well, yes, but—"

Just then Paavo entered the room.

"Here to help, are you?" she asked with more than a hint of sarcasm.

"I'd like to talk to you before dinner, if you've got a minute," Paavo said.

"Excuse me." Brown started to move toward the door.

"Wait." Angie walked over to him and took her tote bag. "Everything's under control here," she said to the two men. "We can all take a ten-minute break. When we get back, though, we'll be very busy. It'll be time to serve the soup, the salad, put the fish on to poach, and season the potatoes. Got it?" Jones nodded. "See you in ten."

With that, she put down the knife and untied her apron.

"You can leave your bag," Jones said. "I'll put it in a corner out of the way. It'll be safe."

"That's okay," Angie said, slinging the bag's long strap over her shoulder. "I want my sunglasses and sunscreen with me. My nose is starting to burn." With that, she followed Paavo out the door.

They walked out onto the deck. It was very

quiet, and they were alone. That was another nice aspect to freighter travel, Angie thought. There were lots of places to go where no one disturbed you.

Paavo placed his hands on her shoulders and gazed steadily into her eyes. "I want to apologize."

A part of her wanted to at least pretend to still be angry with him, just to make him squirm a bit. But one look at his big baby blues and, as usual, she was a goner. Instead of saying anything, she just nodded.

"I've been acting like a son of a bitch ever since this cruise began," he said. "It had to do with my last case. Not you, but I took it out on you."

"I see," she said, still waiting. That wasn't much of an explanation.

"A cop was killed," he said quietly. "It was my fault."

His fault? The raw pain of his words made her stomach knot.

"We were going after a drug lord." He dropped his hands and slid them into his pockets. "Yosh and I connected him to a homicide we were investigating. I had a snitch . . . a guy who was supposed to tell me what was going on. I trusted him. . . ."

Paavo stood behind the police barricade along with his partner, Homicide Inspector Toshiro Yoshiwara, and watched the SWAT team close in on the drug lord's soldiers. The neighborhood appeared deserted; residents here had long ago learned to remain unseen behind barred windows and warped wooden doors that, despite their columns of locks, could be sprung with one sharp kick.

Paavo and Yosh had tracked the gang to the dingy, once-white wooden home in the city's Bayview district. Red and green cement patches lined the fronts of houses instead of lawns. Cracked and chipped cement stairs led to front porches buckling with dry rot.

Their homicide investigation had begun innocuously enough, giving no hint that it would lead to this place. A successful, politically connected lawyer had been killed in what appeared to be a drive-by shooting. Soon, though, the lawyer's use of cocaine had become a prominent factor in the investigation and had led Paavo and Yosh to Jim Nhu, one of the most powerful drug lords in California.

A nervous snitch spilled the location of a drug and money exchange Nhu had planned. The cops and DEA were waiting, ready to move in.

But someone at the drop site, that run-down Bayview house, must have spotted something amiss in the unnaturally quiet neighborhood. A blast of gunfire turned the drug bust deadly. A ten-year veteran of the San Francisco Police Department, Sergeant Ed Gillespie, was hit by the first eruption of bullets. He had stood between Paavo and the drop site. Paavo watched pain and surprise distort the man's beefy features as he fell.

At that moment, more than anything, Paavo wanted Jim Nhu dead. He vowed that Ed Gillespie, a brave man with a wife and family, hadn't died in vain.

An arsenal of M-16's and other automatic weapons held the police at bay for fourteen more hours, until, finally, the gang's firepower diminished and the police pincer formation closed in on the drug dealers.

But something inside Paavo had died along with the police officer. His work had brought the SWAT team to the Bayview house; his work had led to Gillespie's death. Had he overlooked something? Trusted someone he shouldn't have? Been too quick to act and not exercised sufficient caution? He'd carry those questions to his grave.

Suddenly, he knew he was tired of it. Tired of the constant burden of the job, tired of a responsibility too great to handle. Tired of the nightmares after good men die.

He decided to wrap up the case, do all the necessary paperwork, then quit the force.

But the head of the homicide bureau, Lieutenant Hollins, apparently knew him better than he thought. Hollins called him into his office the night the shoot-out ended, the night before he was supposed to go on a vacation he'd forgotten completely about and couldn't bear the thought of. Hollins ordered him to take the vacation.

He had refused, saying he was staying for the funeral and, after finishing up some loose ends, was resigning from the force.

"All the more reason to leave town," Hollins had stated. "You aren't welcome at the funeral."

Paavo could only stare at him, stunned.

Hollins squared his shoulders, his voice, his whole demeanor firm and cold. "Only men who believe in police work—the work Ed Gillespie died doing—are welcome. Not quitters. Take the leave you have scheduled, and when you come back, I'll look at your resignation request."

Yosh had stayed up with Paavo throughout the night talking. The two of them, despite the months they'd worked together, had never talked from the heart the way they did that night.

When morning came, somehow Paavo's bags had been packed, and Yosh had convinced him to go on the cruise with Angie, that there was nothing more he could do in San Francisco. Above all, he needed to get away and think things over.

Paavo drew a deep breath, and as he did, he noticed that Angie's hand held his now, that she had stepped closer to him, and her face had grown pale as he had given her the barest out-line of all that took place that day. "It was my collar. It should have been an easy bust," he said. "But they fired on our guys. I keep wondering what sign I overlooked, what I missed." His voice dropped to a whisper. "Ed Gillespie was right in front of me."

Angie looked away as his words cut through her. Tears filled her eyes at the death of another man, and at Paavo's pain. Her body quaked at the grim reality of his words, but also at the thought that if Gillespie hadn't been there . . . if another man hadn't died . . .

She knew she couldn't say that to Paavo. "I'm sorry," she said, putting her arms around him. "I'm so sorry." There were no platitudes she could give him that would help. Right now, though, what he needed was to feel her hold him. That comfort she *could* give.

"That's why I've got to quit," he said as he stepped back and gazed into her eyes. "When you make a mistake, and another man is killed . . . it simply gets to be too much."

He walked over to the railing and stared out at the sea. "I'm sorry, Angie."

For a while, when they had first come on board and he told her he was leaving the force, she had felt elated. But no longer. Not this way.

If he wanted to leave because he was tired of the danger and the irregular hours, she'd be overjoyed. But he couldn't leave feeling like a failure, feeling that his mistake had caused the death of another.

She walked up behind him and put her arms around his waist, her head against his back. One and a half weeks remained before he would return to work and officially resign. One and a half weeks for her to help him realize that whatever had happened, he'd done what he thought was right. That he was a careful man, meticulous in his police work, who'd never risk anyone's life thoughtlessly. That whatever had made the arrest go all wrong was horrible, but not his fault. Somehow, she'd help him see that.

Yet helping him see that also meant he could change his mind about resigning. He might decide to stay with the police force. And next time, another man might not be there to stop a bullet meant for him.

Could she do that? How could she do otherwise? For all his smiles, he was more unhappy than she'd ever seen him, because this time he doubted himself. The man she'd been vacationing with these past few days wasn't Paavo; he was a shell of the man she loved. She wanted her man back.

He turned to her and brushed her hair back off her face as he looked down at her, then gently kissed her forehead. "Forgive me?" he asked.

"There's nothing to forgive you for," she said, her arms tightening. "I'm glad you told me the whole story. And glad Hollins told you to think about your resignation."

He seemed surprised at her reaction, then he nodded. "I guess your ten minutes are up."

She let go of him. "You're right. I'd better go help the boys with dinner. I'll meet you in the dining room."

"Okay."

She started to turn. "Oh, one last thing. The black-and-blue marks on my arms were caused when someone pulled me into the galley last night, then pushed me into a rack of pots and pans. Be careful."

He grabbed her wrist, stopping her. "Someone did *what?*"

"I don't have time to explain. Actually, there's nothing to explain—I have no idea who it was, or why. Oh, one other thing—would you take my tote bag, please?" she asked. "Having it lying around on the floor while we work seems to bother Mike Jones a lot."

Even more puzzled, he looked from her to the bag. "Sure. I'll hold it."

The meal was every bit the success Angie had hoped it would be. The raves from the passengers and officers were lavish. Even the poached petrale—the fish was so mild Angie decided that's what it had to have been—was praised as a masterpiece.

As the *pot de crème* was served with coffee that Angie had made a little stronger and more robust than usual, Captain Olafson stood and

invited Mike Jones into the dining room for
applause. Jones walked to Angie's side and held
out his hand, pulling her to her feet to stand
beside him. They both took bows to the pleasure and amusement of one and all.

Paavo opened the door to the cabin and stopped dead. To his right, the medicine cabinet was open, and his and Angie's things were out of it and all over the bathroom counter and floor.

In the living room, desk drawers had been opened and cushions pulled off the couch and easy chair. In the bedroom, the bureau drawers had been opened and their contents tossed, and clothes from the closet had been pulled off hangers and lay in a heap on the floor.

"Oh, no!" Angie cried, stepping into the cabin behind him.

"Stay back, Angie," he said. "Let me make sure whoever did this isn't still here."

In no time he did a check, then phoned Julio to get Mr. Johansen.

"My things! Yours!" Angie looked around in a daze. "Paavo, what's going on here?"

He went over to her and put his arm around her shoulders as they slowly went through the cabin. "It'll be okay. We'll find out what's going on. Mr. Johansen will help." The first mate had just stepped into the cabin. Paavo's eyes met his.

"I'll send someone over to clean this up for you," Johansen said, his expression showing how appalled he was by the sight. "Then you can see what's been destroyed or is missing. We'll get to the bottom of whoever is behind this, believe me. I'll not have anyone on my ship . . . uh, on Captain Olafson's ship who is capable of such blatant disregard for the property of others." With that, he stomped out of the room.

When Angie and Paavo turned to watch him leave, they saw Julio and Dudley Livingstone standing in the doorway, taking in everything that had been said.

Mr. Johansen assigned one of the seamen who worked in the engine room to help Julio put the cabin back into shape. When Angie saw the seaman's grease-stained hands and fingernails, she feared he might do more harm to her clothes than being thrown on the floor had done. She joined in to help, and so did Paavo.

It didn't take them long to put the cabin back together again. The only long-lasting damage had been to her toiletries. It seemed everything she'd brought that could be emptied had been—into the sink or the toilet. Whoever heard of a thief with a makeup and lotion fetish? She'd have been happier had he stolen the stuff instead of wasting it.

"Do you believe me now, Paavo?" was all she said after Julio and the seaman left.

"I still don't understand why anyone would think we've got something they want," he said.

"From day one it's been this way, when everything in the bathroom cabinet was pushed around," Angie said, equally puzzled.

"Day one, when the cook ran off the ship and the steward was carried off sick," Paavo mused. "I don't see the connection to us."

"I'm a cook," Angie suggested.

"But the cook left before anyone knew that, and it doesn't explain the steward." Paavo began to pace. "The steward fell ill right outside our cabin . . . was it after he took ill you found your things disturbed?"

"It was that night . . . yes, I think so. Oh! I just remembered that we first saw him out on deck, but then he came indoors. I had assumed he was going to take the elevator down to his cabin, but he didn't. And we had left our door unlocked—just as Mr. Johansen said everyone did while at sea. Ingerson could have easily come in here. He was sick. Maybe he was looking for stomach medicine?"

"Which you keep in full view."

"True."

"That wouldn't explain why someone else came in here."

"You think more than one person searched our things?"

"There's also that bug from the lamp," he added. "If it was a bug. And that whole strange business with your tote bag."

"Actually, Paavo, I'm not sure it was a bug. I mean, I've never seen one except in movies." She didn't want to admit that sometimes she went a bit overboard with her imagination. That might have been one of those times. Or, considering how things were going here, maybe it wasn't.

"Did you talk to anyone about any of this?"

"Only Mr. Johansen. He thought I was just imagining things. He did ask Julio about it, but Julio had already thrown the strange thing away."

"This break-in isn't your imagination. Whatever's going on, someone's becoming more desperate."

"Time to get off the ship, I think," Angie said.

"You're right. Whatever this is about doesn't involve us, I'm sure. It might involve this cabin, though. Anyway, the sooner we get off the ship, the sooner I can go back to practicing being a civilian again."

Angie bit her tongue. She wasn't sure she liked that prospect.

The Hydra entered the galley.

Mike Jones was bending over the sink, scrubbing out a pot used for dinner. What a nice little chef he'd become, she thought. He'd make someone a good husband one of these days.

Maybe even her. She'd have to give that some thought. Probably she was just horny, but it was too dangerous to do anything about it in close quarters like this ship. If anyone walked in on them . . . my, what they'd think!

Mike was certainly good-looking enough to consider marrying. Not as smart as she'd like; but then it was hard, when one had a genius IQ, to find any man who measured up.

What was wrong with her? She hadn't thought about marriage since her days as a debutante, and later at Vassar. She wondered if being around that Amalfi woman had caused it—Amalfi's eyes all but sparkled whenever she looked at her man.

Once she, too, had been that innocent and naive; the world had been her proverbial oyster, waiting for her to pluck its pearl. What a joke. It hadn't taken long for her to learn what life was really about.

"Michael, if I can tear you away from your Comet for a moment . . ."

He spun around. "Oh. I wasn't expecting you." He quickly washed the cleanser off his hands, then grabbed a blue-striped dish towel.

"You failed again, Michael," the Hydra said, leaning back against the sink in the galley.

"Me? Since when is any of this my fault?" He tossed the towel into a corner, just missing her arm.

The Hydra glared at it, at him. "You had her here all day and you couldn't get that stupid tote bag away from her!" She folded her arms. "That bag is our last chance. Since we know the formula isn't in her room, it's got to be in her bag. I want it."

"You had her in the galley last night and did nothing!"

"She didn't have the tote bag with her."

Jones's mouth tightened. "Well, today she had it, but I didn't see you waltz through here and snatch it up as you danced out the door, either!" he said.

"Don't be ridiculous!" She clenched and unclenched her fists. "We arrive in Mazatlán tomorrow, and Colonel Ortega will want his formula. I'll do all I can to hold him off. I just hope he isn't too impatient. If he is, it'll turn ugly fast. He may talk a big line about honor, but he'll slit your throat as soon as look at you. We're going to have to play this carefully."

"You can do it," Jones said.

She lifted one eyebrow, as if wondering whether his words were a compliment or sarcasm.

"It's too bad Amalfi found the bug you left in her room," she said. "I didn't realize you had anything like that."

"A bug?" he asked. "I didn't bug the room."

She stared at him as the full impact of his words hit. "If you didn't, then who did? And why?"

She paced back and forth like a caged animal. "Tell me, can we trust Julio?"

"Julio? What does he have to do with anything?"

"He was friends with Sven. What if Sven gave him the formula? Or what if Sven told him where he put it? Julio keeps hanging around the Amalfi woman. He went in and out of the cabin a number of times carrying those stupid lamps and light bulbs. Maybe Sven put it in her cabin, and Julio used the lamps as a ploy to get in there and pick it up. Maybe Julio put the bug in there himself. Maybe he and Sven planned all along that he'd be involved."

"I can't imagine. What could Julio do with it?"

"The question is, how much did Sven tell him? If this deal falls apart, we can't have any loose ends. We can't have anyone around who might tie us to it. Remember, a man, a scientist, is dead. And the FBI is investigating who killed him."

Mike nodded gravely. "So it's *buenas noches,* Julio, even if he doesn't know a thing."

"We can't take the chance."

"Wait! I've got it! I know where the microfilm is!" Mike faced her, his face filled with excitement. "Ingerson passed it to the cook. That's why Pete Lichty pretended to go nuts and got off the ship so suddenly. It all makes sense. The two were working together."

The Hydra shook her head. "You're completely wrong—as always. I caused Lichty to leave the ship. He was getting too nosy; I'm sure he overheard one of our conversations. He might not ever have put all the pieces together, but I didn't want to take the chance. So, a couple of notes made it clear he'd have to get off the ship or be killed. It was easy—you know how nervous he was to begin with. Finally, a butcher knife stuck into one of his clean aprons drove him over the edge. Almost literally."

"You're sure there wasn't time for Ingerson to have passed it to him before he left?"

"From the time Ingerson stepped on the ship that day to the time Lichty tried to jump off, one or the other was in my view constantly. They didn't have time to meet. Lichty didn't have the nerve to get involved that way, no matter what."

Jones nodded. "You're right about him."

"Of course I am." The Hydra leaned closer. "Now, here's the plan. I want you to do something to the air-conditioning—put a hole in it, remove a part, I don't care. But do something that will stop it from working and will take time to fix. That'll buy us a day or two. Also, it'll mean that the passengers will get off the ship. We'll be able to go through all the cabins once again with a fine-tooth comb. Since Amalfi and Smith will take their things with them to some hotel room, we'll find out which one and take all their belongings. If worse comes to worst, we'll kill them."

"Kill Angie? She hasn't done anything."

"Michael, you are too easily charmed by

women for this business. But maybe they'll be lucky. Maybe we'll find the formula without having to kill them."

"One other question, though," Jones said. "If we break the air-conditioning so the ship can't sail, what if Amalfi and Smith don't want to wait for the repairs and decide to fly to Acapulco right away?"

She shrugged. "If they're dead, they can't go anywhere."

22

"The ship is not here yet!" Colonel Hector Ortega exclaimed, climbing out of his limousine almost before it stopped. Instead of the freighter he'd hoped to see out in the bay, only seagulls greeted him. A vendor rolled his noisy *churro* cart nearby. The colonel whirled about and glared as he passed.

Elsewhere, Acapulco harbor was abuzz with people, boats, cars, and cargo, but the area where the freighters came in, where containers were loaded and unloaded, was quiet as death.

"Damn! I thought you fixed it so it would not stop at Cabo San Lucas." Despite the harsh, tropical sun, Ortega took off his sunglasses, hoping to spot the approaching ship on the horizon. But the sea was empty of anything larger than fishing boats.

"I started to, but someone had beaten me to

141

it, my colonel. It will get here soon," Eduardo
said. "The harbormaster is expecting it. An hour
or two, even a day or more, does not mean anything in a freighter's schedule."

"I am sick of waiting," Ortega roared. "If
someone beat you, it must be her, the Hydra.
Why would she want the ship to arrive here
early, before I expect it? Does she plan a surprise? I do not like such surprises. Perhaps I
need to plan a little surprise for her!"

"Let us go to the restaurant across the street.
We will have something cold to drink, a little
something to eat. It will make the time go faster
for you."

"Yes, you are right, as always, Eduardo." The
colonel and Eduardo got back into the limousine and the chauffeur drove them the few feet
across the boulevard to a restaurant.

George Gresham took off his straw hat and
laid it on top of the *churro* cart, then ran into a
telephone booth outside the harbormaster's
office and quickly dialed a number. "He's at
the harbor," he said without even identifying
himself. "He's looking for the freighter. It's
due anytime now." He didn't mention hearing
the name Hydra. He'd keep that little bit of
explosive news under his hat for now. He
didn't want to sound as if he was going overboard on this.

He listened. "He's gone into a fancy restaurant, but there's a cantina, Fernando's, with out-

side tables. I think we should all meet there. We can wait and watch. We know how to do that, don't we?" He laughed so hard his fake mustache fell off.

"Okay," he said after a while. "I'll be waiting."

23

"Yoo-hoo, Mr. Johansen," Nellie Nebler called. "My cabin is growing awfully warm."

"There is a problem with the air-conditioning," the first mate replied.

"Problem, indeed!" Livingstone snorted. "My dear sir, it isn't working at all." Dressed as always in a white suit, he rapidly fanned his face with his white Panama hat. "When will it be fixed?"

Catching part of the conversation, Angie and Paavo walked out to the main deck to hear the first mate's explanation of the sudden heat in the cabin.

"A part is broken," Johansen admitted. "The engineer needs to replace it. If no replacement is available in Mazatlan—and we doubt any will be—one will be air-freighted to us in a day or two."

"Gracious," Nellie cried.

"Two days? In this heat?" Livingstone was

shouting now. "That's intolerable."

"There's much about freighter travel that is
not for the faint of heart," Johansen said.
"When I began, there was no such thing as air-
conditioning. The sea is a natural air conditioner."

"But not when the freighter is sitting docked
in a tropical port!" Livingstone bellowed.

"If you are uncomfortable, you can always get
a hotel in town for a couple of nights. You must
not expect us to reimburse you, though."
Johansen's jaw was set, his voice never rising
above a monotone. "We are making your accommodations available to you, as always. If you
choose not to use them, that is between you and
your pocketbook. It isn't this shipping line's
concern."

"But you've made the air-conditioning fail!"
Nellie cried.

"We have not, Mrs. Nebler," Johansen began
patiently. "Mechanical parts fail now and then.
Before you signed up for this cruise, you were
warned that changes from planned itineraries
often occur in freighter travel. This is one such
change."

"Let's go," Angie said to Paavo, turning away
from the confrontation. "I've heard enough.
Let's just pack our bags and fly, or rent a car, or
even take a bus, to Acapulco. I want off."

"I agree."

"I'll join you," Livingstone said, hurrying
after them.

Angie couldn't believe he intended to go with them.

"We're going to Acapulco," Angie explained.

"Transportation will take time to organize," Livingstone said. "In the meantime, I know a very nice hotel here in Mazatlán. It's in the old part of the city—lots of charm, away from the modern tourist sector. That's where I'm staying. You should take a room there, too, and see how things work out on board. Johansen said the problem might be fixed sometime tomorrow. No need to give up your cruise so hastily."

"There's nothing hasty—" Angie began.

"Let's talk to the man," Paavo said, his gaze never leaving Livingstone's.

"Excellent," Livingstone replied. The three of them walked into the lounge, where it was a little cooler, at least, than the humid outside air.

Livingstone led them to a secluded table in a far corner of the room. They sat. "Now," Paavo said, leaning close to Livingstone, "what's this about?"

Angie looked with surprise from one man to the other. The way they spoke and regarded each other had changed perceptibly. She didn't know why.

Livingstone sat straighter in his chair, his jaw firmer. Gone was the lackadaisical art collector. "What I'm going to tell you must never be repeated." Even his voice took on a harder edge. His eyes quickly scanned the surroundings before he continued. "I trust you, Inspector

Smith, because you are, I have learned, an officer of the law of some distinction and repute, and I trust your lady because . . . well, because she is your lady."

Paavo's calm expression showed he'd expected that Livingstone wasn't what he seemed on the surface. But Angie hadn't imagined anything like that at all.

Livingstone took a deep breath. "I fear that if you leave Mazatlán, your lives may be in danger."

"*What?*" Angie exclaimed.

"I work for Interpol. We've suspected for some time that this ship has been in some way connected with people who transfer . . . hmm, let's call it information . . . from one person or group in one country to those in another."

Paavo glanced at Angie. "Just where did your cousin learn about this freighter?"

"I don't know," she said, swallowing hard.

"In any event," Livingstone continued. "Our friends in the FBI recently contacted us and told us they feared that a professor who had been working on a special U.S. government project had decided to sell his discovery to an international consortium. The FBI was watching him, but somehow the professor was murdered, and his formula and all the files he had on how to develop it were deleted. They had no idea how the deed was done."

"That was Professor Von Mueller?" Paavo asked.

"Precisely. This ship was in the Bay Area when the formula was stolen. Since we'd been interested in everything happening on the ship, when Sven Ingerson was taken off, his photo was obtained by Interpol. On a hunch, we showed it to the FBI. It turns out that the FBI agent who had been watching the professor recognized Sven as a street musician the professor had given some money to in Berkeley. Apparently, the professor occasionally gave these street people money, so the FBI hadn't thought much of it."

"Oh, my God," Angie murmured. Not that she understood much about the FBI or Interpol. But she did understand that her quiet, crime-free vacation had evaporated.

"You're saying," Paavo said, his elbows on the table, all his attention on Livingstone, "that the professor may have given Ingerson the missing formula? But then Ingerson got sick. Legitimately sick, do you think? Or does it seem someone wanted to get rid of him?"

Angie's head swiveled to Paavo. He was following this . . . and seemed interested. Whatever happened to civilian life?

"Apparently it's legitimate," Livingstone replied. "Botulism. We haven't heard of anyone playing around with botulism as a poison. But I guess anything is possible."

Angie shuddered. Botulism was a cook's worst nightmare, though easy to guard against with proper care.

"Once we learned about Ingerson," Livingstone went on, "we were pretty sure the formula would be found on this ship. A few strings were pulled to get me on board to find out all I could. I'm glad I did."

"What's the formula for?" Paavo asked.

"Sorry. Classified. But believe me, it's big. It can change the course of world history."

"That's hard to believe," Angie said. "What could possibly do that?"

"I can't tell you," Livingstone said.

"Let's back up," Paavo said. "Whatever the formula is, if Ingerson had it and he's now off the ship, what's the problem and how are we involved?"

"Ingerson was just a courier," Livingstone explained. "The brains behind all of this is a woman. We don't know her real name. We don't even have a picture of her. But everyone who has ever worked with her calls her the Hydra."

"Hydra? From mythology?" Paavo asked.

"A many-headed beast," Angie said, glad to contribute something.

Livingstone continued. "Instead of many heads, our Hydra has many disguises. We aren't certain that she's on the *Valhalla*—but she might be. In any event, whoever is on the ship and involved in this situation seems to think the formula is in your possession. Again, I don't know why. But that has to be the reason why your room and your belongings have been searched."

"But once they were searched and nothing found, this . . . Hydra . . . should know we don't have the formula. She should forget about us," Angie said hopefully.

"Or," Livingstone countered, "she thinks she hasn't done a thorough enough search. The timing of the sudden breakdown of the air conditioner is suspicious."

"Agreed," Paavo said. "That and the fact that there didn't seem to be any dockworkers' strike in Cabo San Lucas."

"I called to check on that strike," Livingstone said. "As you suspected, it was bogus. It made me think that someone didn't want any of us— and especially not you—to get off in Cabo. Looking at the alternative, it's also possible that someone wants you, or all of us, to stay in Mazatlán for a while."

"This sounds like something James Bond should be involved in," Angie said, her head swimming. "You're just speculating. Both of you."

"That's true," Livingstone admitted. "But your belongings have been searched, and so far your persons have not been in danger. I believe the safest thing for you to do is to allow these people to get their hands on your luggage at will. As I mentioned, I can recommend a small hotel. The owner is discreet—I've already talked to him. He's holding two rooms for us that are across the hall from each other. You can spend tonight there comfortably. By the time the ship is tied down and you go through customs, it'll be fairly late, and I can't imagine anything would happen. But tomorrow, be sure you leave the room early and don't return until nightfall. Sightsee or whatever else you want to do—as long as you stay away from that room. If someone comes to inspect your luggage, I'll be there to catch them. It's really extraordinarily simple."

"But something might go wrong," Paavo said. "I'm not putting Angie in danger."

"What could happen?" Livingstone sounded completely confident. "Of course there are risks. Objectively, the worst thing would be if no one shows up to inspect your bags. In that case, I sail off on the *Valhalla* when it leaves Mazatlán, and you can fly to Acapulco and continue your vacation. It's only for one day—that's all I'm asking."

"Angie's a civilian," Paavo said. "I can't let her get involved."

Livingstone folded his hands. "Interpol has been after the Hydra for ten years. She's been a constant thorn in our side. Nothing major, just lots of little, niggling annoyances. Usually, the people she's killed—"

"Killed?" Angie cried. "That's a niggling annoyance?"

"Those people were the sort where, to be frank, we didn't know whether to punish or commend her for their deaths. But this time is different. The victim was a professor, a chemist. A bit too avaricious, perhaps, but that's not a capital offense. Killing him was. All I'm asking is

one night's lodging—two at most—to help
Interpol and your government. After all, it *is* the
government's formula. How can you say no?"

"It doesn't sound that dangerous," Angie said
to Paavo.

"You're both wrong. It's not going to be that
easy," Paavo said. "You've already said this Hydra
is dangerous and has eluded you for years. You
can't believe she'd be so stupid as to walk into a
trap now."

"She has no reason to suspect anything.
You're seeing ghosts where there are none," Livingstone insisted.

The look that filled Paavo's eyes for the slight-
est moment told her Livingstone was right—
ghosts were bothering Paavo, were making him
even more cautious and worried than usual.
"You need a backup," Paavo said to the other
man. "You're putting yourself in too much danger."

"A backup? For this? I had no idea you Yanks
had grown so tender. I can do a job like this with
my eyes closed—and believe me, they'll be
open. It's child's play."

"No," Paavo insisted. "You've got to—"

"Stop. I'm an Interpol agent. I know this terri-
tory; I know these people," Livingstone said.
"What you need to think very hard about is that,
if the air-conditioning breakdown was rigged, it
could only mean that the Hydra doesn't want
you, us, or the ship to leave Mazatlán. If you try
to leave, she might decide to stop you. That, my

friends, is when this little affair could become very dangerous indeed."

"Paavo?" Angie said, unable to hide the worry in her voice.

He looked from her to Livingstone, his eyes grim and determined. "Where's the hotel?"

24

"You're really going to leave the ship, dearie?" Nellie asked.

"Yes," Angie answered loud enough even for Harold Cockburn to hear her with his hearing aid turned down. "We're going to the Hotel del Sud. We'll be back when the ship's repaired, I guess."

"Be careful out there," Nellie cried. "We're staying on board ourselves."

"I thought you wanted to leave," Angie said.

"We changed our minds. Anyway, the cabin's paid for, even if it is a tad warm."

A tad? "Okay. We'll see you in a day or so," Angie said as Paavo and Julio appeared on deck with their bags. "Bye."

"So long, dearie," Nellie said.

When they reached the bottom of the gangway, Julio steered them toward customs and the harbormaster's office, where they had to show

their papers before being allowed into the
country. Paavo gave Julio a tip and Julio gave
them his best wishes, glancing longingly toward
Angie before he hurried away.

"Mazatlán might not be so bad after all,"
Paavo muttered, watching the retreating steward.

"I'm sorry, I couldn't hear you," Angie said.

"Nothing," he replied. As they lined up to
show their papers, he turned to her and spoke
in a normal tone. "Back on the ship, what was all
the shouting about with Nellie?"

"Just wanted to be sure *everyone* knew where
we were staying—in case what Livingstone said
was true," she explained.

Paavo had to suppress a grin. As always with
Angie, when she got involved with something,
she went at it full tilt.

The constant whirring of the outdoor fans at
Fernando's, a small, inexpensive cantina across
from the Mazatlán harbor, suggested that they
were spinning at full speed, even if all it meant
was that they were merely pushing the hot,
humid air around a bit. To the patrons at the
cluster of sidewalk tables, some breeze was better than none at all.

At one table, a woman fanned herself with a
round, palm-leaf-shaped fan with a bamboo
handle. It didn't help. The three men with her
looked equally miserable. None of them spoke.

The woman sipped her sangria, the men their

beers. A plate of *buñuelos* sat in the center of the table, uneaten, a victim of the hot, miserable weather. Three colorfully dressed street musicians circled their table and began wildly strumming their guitars.

The American, George Gresham, cringed. He recognized the musical introduction. The whole world probably recognized that introduction. He gritted his teeth and tried not to look too pained.

Sure enough, the loud, slightly off-key strains of "La Bamba" began to fill the air, and all the other customers' eyes turned to the four of them. To Gresham's horror, Grundil Duchievor was smiling at the musicians and rocking her head as if she was enjoying it. When they began the *"Ba-ba-bamba"* chorus, in voices louder than he thought humanly possible, he fished in his pockets for some money and practically threw it into the hands of one of the men.

"Thank you. Thank you," the man said. When they didn't leave, George stood up. "*Gracias* and good-bye."

The lead musician nodded and walked off, singing as he went. The others followed.

Grundil lifted one eyebrow and peered coldly at George. A tall, thin woman with sharply angled cheekbones, she rapped a pack of Gauloises against her forefinger. "Vhy did you send them avay, George?" she asked. Her voice was deep, almost masculine. She freed one of the unfiltered cigarettes.

"Why not? Why would we want them singing Richie Valens to us?" he asked.

"I liked it," she said, lifting her head imperiously, her pencil-sharp nose pointing toward the street, carefully eyeing the passers-by. Somewhere in her forties, she was tall and slinky, with hazel eyes, black eyebrows penciled to wing up and outward, and straight, jet-black hair worn in a chin-length blunt cut with deep, straight bangs. Her long fingers, tipped by square-cut unmanicured nails, held her cigarette at a rigid angle while she lit it. Inhaling deeply, she tossed back her head and harshly blew a long plume of smoke into the air.

"At least it's better than 'Guantanamera,'" said her husband, Béla. A short, pudgy man, he had thinning black hair and large, protruding black eyes. His voice, high and nasal, was the complete opposite of his wife's.

George decided he'd have to think about that possibility.

Whenever a new group of foreign tourists sat down, the musicians surrounded them and sang "La Bamba" again. George lost count after about the eighth time, glad there was nothing handy that was sharp and could fit in his ear.

No one at the table spoke. Not him, or Grundil Duchievor, or her husband, Béla. And especially not Shawn MacDougall.

George looked at the fourth man in their party, stiff and formal, dressed in a V-necked blue sweater, white shirt, red bow tie, gray slacks, slick-soled black moccasins, and binoculars around his neck. It's amazing he didn't pass out in the heat.

Shawn was Chinese. Somehow, someone in the Chinese embassy in Beijing had screwed up royally when putting together a phony foreign passport for the guy, back during the last days of the cold war, when things like that were common and the Chinese weren't the heavy players they were now. They weren't nearly as sophisticated in their espionage back then, and George figured some poor clerk was just pulling out Western-style names, trying to anglicize the Chinese spy's real name—Xian Mah-dong. What he evidently hadn't understood was that there was a big difference between anglicizing a name and scotticizing it.

MacDougall had been stuck with the ridiculous moniker ever since.

Not that it mattered anymore. Hell, nothing any of them did mattered anymore. The cold war was over and they were has-beens. George was a has-been at only fifty-five. He had plenty of years left, too. Good years. But what with downsizing in the spy industry . . . and those few who were left had to know all that high-tech garbage. Give him the good old days! The John le Carré days, when being a spy meant you were tough, a man alone—a modern-day cowboy doing good, fighting evil.

He batted away a fly.

Now being a spy meant you got involved in

industrial espionage. How boring! He almost felt sorry for the young guys just entering the business. Almost.

But the four of them—the not-so-old-timers—had once been good. More than good. Great. They used to have a lot of fun spying on each other, in fact. That was how they had met years ago, first in Berlin, then Prague, and finally a stint in Albania. That should have warned all of them that the end was near. Even the name Albania made him shudder.

Then Shawn was bounced from his job, the Duchievors lost their government, and he'd been downsized into an early retirement.

They'd found each other again in Mazatlán by chance, all looking for cheap housing in a warm climate. So they teamed up. It had seemed natural enough. Retirement and the end of wars made strange bedfellows.

They had spent their careers sitting and watching. It's what they were used to doing, liked doing, in fact. So they sat in cantinas much like this one and watched.

"There—look at those two. The big bruiser and the dish who's with him. What a babe," George Gresham said, watching the people from the ship go through customs.

Shawn MacDougall keyed into his personal organizer. The small, battery-operated computer was as high-tech as any of them were these days. "The records Grundil lifted from the harbormaster show them to be either Nellie and

Marvin Neblar, Ruby and Harold Cockburn, or Angelina Amalfi and Paavo Smith."

"It's the last two," Grundil said. "He doesn't treat her as if she vere a vife. He's being too much the gentleman."

"But Grundil, I am alvays the gentleman vith you," Béla said.

She sneered, and continued watching. "Ah! Look. She is talking to a very handsome young man. He's dressed in white—he must be the ship's steward."

"But the guy she was with is sneaking away from them," George said. "He's heading for a phone booth. Whoa-ho-ho! Suspicious-city, USA! They're the ones, gang."

"What could they be up to?" MacDougall mused.

"They don't look like the type to deal vith a dictator-vannabe," Grundil said, squinting mightily. It wasn't that her eyesight was going bad. It was the constant haze in Mazatlán—it made things hard to see sometimes. Especially if they were too far away or too close up. "Ortega never had the *cojones* to make a big man of himself."

"Maybe," Béla said breathlessly, "vorking vith classy people like them, this time he vill. And ve vill find out about it and varn everyone. Then our reputations vill be restored."

"And if not," George added, "we might at least find a way to get some money out of it so we can retire somewhere that's not so hot or humid. Like, maybe, Juneau."

25

Paavo didn't like the idea of leaving Angie at the lascivious mercy of Julio Rodriguez, but there were times, like now, when it was a lot easier than explaining to her what he was up to. He hurried to a pay phone and put in a call to his partner, Yoshiwara.

"Paavo?" Yosh sounded shocked. "Hey, partner, good to hear from you. But aren't you supposed to be taking it easy on a cruise?"

Yosh was Mr. Congeniality, a walking contradiction to the stereotypical dour, serious homicide inspector. Since Paavo was dour and serious enough for both of them, the two men had a good partnership.

"How did it go Tuesday?" Paavo asked softly, thinking about the funeral.

"Hey, what can I say? It went."

"And I'm on some damned cruise. I should have been there."

"No, pal. It wouldn't have helped. Rest, realize you did everything you could, then get the hell back here and help me out with these damn cases. I got one case, the guy was found in his apartment, deadbolts up one side and down the other on the front door, and safety bars on the windows, also locked. He was found shot in the back of the head."

"Sounds like suicide," Paavo said drily.

"Yeah. You're right," Yosh admitted.

"I've got a job for you," Paavo said, going straight to the reason he had called.

"A job? Wait a minute. You're supposed to be on vacation. You aren't sitting around thinking about some murder case, are you? Ed Gillespie's killers are behind bars. They aren't going nowhere. We've got everything under control. Now relax, fellow."

"This job has to do with my vacation. I need you to check out some people. The other passengers, to begin with."

"Are you kidding me? How many are there?"

"Only five. We're on a freighter, remember?"

"That's right. Leave it to you, partner, to find some rough-and-tumble way to take a cruise. With a fancy woman like Angie, too. Okay, who are these people?"

Paavo gave him the passengers' names.

After writing them down, Yosh said, "Can I ask why you want me to check up on them?"

"There's something odd going on here. I can't begin to figure it out."

"Dangerous?"

Good question. "I'm not sure," Paavo said. "I hope not."

"Okay, pal. I'll run all the usual checks. Give me a couple of days."

"That's too long. I need to know right away. Tomorrow, this same time."

"I'll do my best." Yosh sounded a little skeptical of how successful his best might be. "Say, where are you now?"

"Mazatlán."

"Mazatlán? You're making pretty good time, aren't you?"

"The freighter couldn't stop at Cabo San Lucas. We were supposed to spend a couple of days there. But I'm not done—I want you to check on a few more people."

"Why didn't I guess?"

"One of the stewards got sick and had to leave the ship. Find out how he's doing, will you? Sven Ingerson. Whenever we ask, we're told no one knows how he is, which is hard to believe. They probably took him to an emergency hospital in or near Long Beach."

"Got it."

"The cook, Peter Lichty, jumped ship in Oakland—"

"He *was* desperate."

"See what you can find out about him."

"Okay."

"And last, do the same for a professor who was found dead in Berkeley. Professor Conrad Von Mueller."

"Will do, partner. Anything else you'd like me to do? Check up on the crew of the Queen Mary, maybe?"

"That'll do it."

"Thank God." Then Yosh laughed. "Remind me never to take a vacation with you, okay?"

Even in November the tropical, humid heat was a shock. Angie took out a handkerchief and pressed it to her cheeks and forehead but didn't say a word. She wasn't one to complain. Much.

As they drove along Avenida Olas Altas, she asked the driver to stop and wait a minute, then jumped out and ran up to an ATM machine. Paavo watched in amazement as she put in a credit card and got back nearly two hundred dollars' worth of Mexican pesos at the push of a button. He should have thought of that, even though he never bothered with ATMs in San Francisco and hadn't traveled outside the country in years. Earlier, Julio had offered to exchange a hundred dollars for him before he left the ship. He had agreed, and despite Julio's unfavorable exchange rate, he was willing to concede that Julio might, in fact, have had a few good qualities. Now, though, he wasn't so sure.

"I didn't know you knew Spanish," he said when she got back into the cab.

"I don't. But I do speak Italian and French—and I know some prayers in Latin. They're all close enough that I can, to a degree, fake it."

"I'm impressed." He meant it.

Before long, he saw a small hotel with a placard showing Hotel del Sud, and an ENGLISH SPOKEN HERE sign in the window.

Badly in need of paint, the building had a pinkish tone, with narrow wooden balconies on the upper floors. The wood looked weak, as if the balconies were for show, not for anyone to actually stand on. Blue full-length shutters covered the windows.

"I don't know about this," Angie said softly.

"Stop here," Paavo said to the cab driver.

As the two of them lifted all of Angie's luggage from the trunk, she picked up her tote bag and carry-on and went ahead into the hotel.

Dark wooden and rattan furnishings filled the lobby. A wide-bladed ceiling fan blew hot, humid air around the room. Angie felt as if she'd just stepped into an Indiana Jones movie.

The hotelier, though, won her over with his warm greeting. He was a transplanted Australian, helpful in a salty, carefree manner. He quickly sent a bellboy out to help Paavo.

They were shown their room, a second floor walk-up. It was small, with thick white walls and dark wood trim. The furniture might have been referred to as expensive Mission style back in the United States, but here, it was heavy, utilitarian, and old. A large crucifix hung over the bed. There was no air conditioning.

Angie walked into the room and collapsed onto a stiff, straight-back wooden chair beside a small writing table. Her hair was a mess, her clothes were a mess, and her nails were a mess.

But she didn't care. She was on dry land.

Angie watched Paavo undress and go into the bathroom to take a shower, about the only way to cool off in the hot, humid weather. His mood had taken a turn for the better since he'd become involved with Livingstone. He wasn't yet 100 percent, but things were better.

As she listened to the water running, she got an idea. In no time, she'd peeled the sweaty, clinging clothes from her body and padded into the bathroom.

"Hi," she said, peeking around the shower curtain that covered the bathtub. Paavo held soap in one hand, a washcloth in the other. His eyes showed surprise, then something deep, almost primal, as he put the washcloth down and held out his hand to her.

She stepped into the tub. He drew her toward him, until they were both standing under the cooling spray.

That shower went from cooling spray to the hottest, longest, most satisfying steambath she'd ever taken.

*   *   *

They lay on the bed, drying off and catching their breaths again. After a while, Angie turned to Paavo. "Hungry?" she asked.

"Not anymore." He trailed his fingers along her spine.

"I meant for dinner."

"There's probably a restaurant near the hotel," he said. "We could go find one."

"I think the last decent meal we ate was the dinner I cooked," she said. On board ship, they'd slept through breakfast, and by lunchtime the air conditioner had broken. Although fruit and sandwiches were put on the table, everyone had been too hot and miserable to eat.

"You're right," he said. "Over twenty-four hours ago."

"No wonder I'm starving."

He threw back the sheet. "Let's get ready and go."

A short while later, they left the hotel and walked along a narrow street filled with shops and sidewalk vendors. Angie could see Paavo looking over his shoulder, peering into doorways and side streets. She smiled to herself. Her cop was nearly back.

On the corner they found a small restaurant called El Toro, which had both an indoor and outdoor eating area. Livingstone sat at one of the tables, a glass of beer before him, and used his hat to fan himself. Although he was clearly aware of them, he looked through them as if

he'd never seen them before. They weren't sure
what he was up to, but went along with his pre-
tense.

Inside, the restaurant was fairly empty except
for two tables with families. Angie and Paavo sat
at a table and placed their orders. They began
with an appetizer of *sierra ceviche*, a dish made by
using a lime juice marinade to essentially "cook"
shredded mackerel, and then the fish was
mixed with minced avocado, tomato, and chili
peppers, plus cilantro and olive oil. After that,
since Mazatlán is one of the shrimp capitals of
the world, Angie ordered grilled shrimp spiced
a la diablo. Paavo, instead, looked over the list-
ing of fish he almost never saw in San Francisco
and decided on smoked marlin—*marlin ahu-
mada*. Curious though he was, he took a pass on
the turtle soup after Angie assured him there
was nothing "mock" about it.

A short while later, two men and a rather
exotic-looking woman entered the restaurant
and sat at the table next to theirs.

How could one person have so many clothes?
Five pieces of coordinated Fendi luggage were
stacked in the corner, along with two pieces of
utilitarian Samsonite. George Gresham was surprised they hadn't unpacked anything yet. Most
women were compulsive about wrinkles, in their
clothes as well as on their faces, and unpacked
as soon as they arrived anyplace—which helped
the former problem, if not the latter.

He stooped over and used a laser detector on the top Fendi piece to search for any devices rigged up to the case that might harm him or let the woman know her bag had been tampered with. Nothing showed up on his scope. Okay. That meant either that she wasn't using anything special or that the laser didn't work.

Or she was just a casual tourist.

But he wasn't about to take any chances. Not when, first, Colonel Ortega, a known underworld figure, had mentioned the Hydra being on the *Valhalla;* second, his old friends back at FBI headquarters seemed convinced the Hydra was headed toward Mazatlán; and third, this little woman had suddenly shown up—off the *Valhalla,* in Mazatlán, and right here in a hotel known to the spy trade.

Two plus two. Tic plus tac. Quid plus quo. She had to be the Hydra.

Quickly he picked open the luggage and went through it all. Nothing. Well, that didn't surprise him. The Hydra was too clever to leave anything incriminating in a suitcase. But he had to check, nonetheless. That's what he'd been trained to do, what he'd spent years doing, in fact.

Just wait until the boys back in Quantico learned that he, old retired George, was the one who'd finally captured the Hydra. Yessir. That he alone had been able to do the job where all others had failed. They'd gotten close, but she'd beaten them. They'd never even seen her face.

But he had. That very afternoon, as she and
the guy she ran around with—a bodyguard?—
checked into the hotel. He'd followed them and
found out which one was their room. They
never even noticed. He was that good.

He flipped through a small address book
she'd left in one of her suitcases. What was it supposed to be for? Sending postcards back home?
He laughed. The Hydra, sending postcards!

The book had her name and address on the
first page. He assumed it was there as identification in case she lost it—as if anyone would ever
bother to return a lost address book. Talk about
a holdover from past times. These days, people
would as soon shoot you as return anything
you'd lost. Angelina Amalfi, it said. San Francisco. Yep. It was his considered opinion that she
was most definitely the Hydra. Angelina Amalfi
was a made-up name if ever he heard one.

He lifted his hat and rubbed his crew-cut
blond hair.

For twenty years his opinion had always been
on target—and valued. That was why he'd held
his position for so long. Now his opinion had
led him straight to the Hydra.

Some people said she wasn't so clever. But he
knew better. As far as he was concerned, she was
the cleverest, most deadly perpetrator of industrial espionage in the world. At least that was
sure as hell what he would tell the press after he
captured her.

But . . . captured her for what? He couldn't

just arrest her for no reason. Not even active FBI agents could do that, let alone retired ones.

He had to find out what she was up to.

He checked his watch. In his excitement, he seemed to have lost track of time. He hadn't been in the room too long, had he? He'd come up here as soon as he saw Amalfi and her friend enter the restaurant. His friends were supposed to keep her busy. He sure hoped they hadn't finked out on him.

Perspiration broke out on his forehead. What if she wasn't hungry? What if she'd just wanted a drink and was even now on her way back? He had to get out of here.

Good God! Footsteps. In the hall. He froze for just an instant, then his old training kicked in and he crawled under the bed. He hoped she hadn't heard him sneeze from all the dust balls.

But the footsteps continued past the room. Slowly, cautiously, he crawled out again.

With his heart pounding so hard he was afraid he wouldn't hear the Hydra if she did come back, he pulled the smoke detector out of his backpack. It wasn't actually a smoke detector, of course, but a tiny camera—one that connected via remote control to a receiver in his room. Or so he hoped. He'd "borrowed" it in Quantico upon learning he was being down-and-out-sized and hadn't even unpacked it until now.

He held the miniature instrument in his hand. Where to put it? On the back, peel-off paper covering a sticky substance meant he could put it just about anywhere. He looked at it uncertainly.

Research and Development had assured the FBI it would work. R&D cost taxpayers plenty with little toys like this. It sure as hell better work.

There was a large armoire in the room, the doors pushed all the way open, revealing shelves. He could put it on the top shelf, where extra blankets were placed for guests. No one would be using an extra blanket in this heat. But the gizmo looked like a smoke detector.

He didn't want it on the ceiling, where it'd look down in just one spot. He wanted a view of the room. He stuck it to the wall above the armoire, angling it as best he could toward the bed. That was probably where most of the action would go on in the room, anyway. So he took in a little cheesecake—so what? Of course, if the Hydra found out he'd been watching her in bed . . . The thought of what she might do to him made him dizzy.

26

Angie's first thought was that the woman looked like someone out of a French *film noir*. Except that this wasn't a film. This was Mazatlán.

The woman had left her friends and glided over to their table. She was at least five feet ten inches tall and wore a formfitting, long-sleeved black jersey dress that reached to mid-calf. Her shoes had thick, chunky heels with ankle straps. Without a word, she oozed into a spare chair across from Paavo.

"You are foreigners," she said, her voice a deep contralto, her words slightly accented in the distinctive Central European style of Gabor or Lugosi.

"We are," Angie said, wondering what this crazy scheme they'd agreed to was going to turn up next. Livingstone hadn't mentioned anything about other people being involved. "We're Americans."

"I know. I could tell just by looking at you."
Her gaze inched slowly over Angie, matching
her deliberate, slightly menacing way of speaking. "Your clothes, your style."

Angie looked down at her Gianni Versace
dress and Ferragamo shoes. *Oh, really?* she
thought.

"I take it you aren't an American," Paavo said.
Angie smirked.

"You are correct. My name is Grundil Duchievor. All of us"—she pointed to the table where
the two men sat, and they nodded—"are staying at the same hotel as you, and ve noticed
you sitting here alone, so I came to say hello. To
be . . . friendly."

"I'm Angie Amalfi, and this is Paavo Smith."
Angie wanted to show she could be friendly herself, even if the woman did seem a bit peculiar.

"How nice to meet you," Grundil said.

"I've never heard the name Grundil before,"
Angie said. "What kind of name is that?"

"I vould have said I vas Transylvanian, vonce
upon a time. Now I have no country." Her smile
had a strangely unnerving effect on Angie. It
was like being smiled at by a skeleton.

"Oh. I see," Angie said. Just then, the two
men who had been seated with Grundil rose,
moved to the table, and stood there silently, just
staring at her and Paavo.

"This is my husband, Béla," Grundil said, gesturing toward a short, chubby man wearing a
dark brown suit, a white shirt, and a yellow tie,

who, upon being introduced, thrust out a pudgy hand to Paavo.

"Ve are most pleased to make your acquaintance," he said in a high, nasal voice.

"My name is Xian, I mean, MacDougall," said a soft voice in a completely different accent. "I mean Shawn MacDougall," he hastily corrected himself.

She looked past Béla to see a Chinese man bow with great formality in her direction. *Shawn MacDougall?* Who was he trying to kid? He wore a starched white shirt, blue bow tie, gray sweater, and black slacks. Angie was as amazed by his outfit as by his name. Didn't these people feel the heat in here?

"Hello, Mr. MacDougall?" She couldn't stop her voice from rising on the last syllable, turning her statement into a question.

"I'm fine, thank you," he said, somewhat inappropriately.

Paavo held out his hand to him. "Hello."

The poor man looked ready to sink through the floor with embarrassment, then turned and hurried back to his own table, where he gulped some water.

Béla peered up at his tall wife, his bulging eyes nearly popping from their sockets. "I didn't know he vas so shy," he said, more whiny-sounding than ever.

"Or maybe something else," Grundil replied darkly. Both cast their dark eyes on Angie and Paavo, then shut their mouths tightly.

Just then a newcomer entered the restaurant and headed directly toward their table.

A fellow American, Angie thought wryly, all the way from his yellow cotton hat, festooned with fish lures, down to his blue canvas deck shoes. He pulled off the hat, revealing a crew cut and steely blue eyes. He wore a short-sleeved green oxford shirt, buttoned to his muscular neck, and blue Dockers.

"Hi there, Grundil, Béla. Won't you introduce me to your new friends?"

"This is another American, George Gresham," Grundil said.

"A couple of Yanks. Great," George greeted them.

"Why don't both of you join us?" Paavo said to George and Béla, who was still standing. Mac-Dougall continued to sit alone at his own table.

Béla sat beside Grundil while George grabbed a chair from the table behind them and swung it around next to Angie. "It's pretty quiet in here," he said. "Did I interrupt something?"

"Nothing at all," Grundil said. "Ve vere just starting to get to know von another."

"Oh, great. So tell me, where you from in the States?"

They kept up the inconsequential chatter for nearly an hour before Angie and Paavo excused themselves. As they left, Angie realized that they had discussed plenty about her, little about Paavo, and nothing at all about the four strangers.

*   *   *

George Gresham leaned back against the head-board in his room, a bottle of *cerveza* at his side. It had taken him only a half hour to get the TV set up so he could pull in the picture from the little camera in the Hydra's bedroom. It was just like one of those security devices in a depart-ment store. He could sit here and watch just about every move the Hydra and her friend made.

This was going to be great! He'd left the restaurant moments after they did, stopping at an *abacería* only long enough to buy a beer. He turned on the TV as soon as he entered his room—and it worked. It hadn't been all that dif-ficult to set up, either.

He grinned from ear to ear as he watched the Hydra walking around her room, every detail as clear as if he'd been right there with her. God, but he was good!

She was good, too, he had to admit. She hadn't stumbled once when answering ques-tions during dinner tonight. She'd sounded as sweet and innocent as any dumb tourist. Little did she know that he was on to her.

Now she was unpacking her suitcases. Putting clothes in the closet after shaking out the wrin-kles. Yep, just like a woman. God, he was even better than good!

Whenever she carried a blouse or sweater or underwear toward the camera, the picture was so clear he could see the length of her eye-

lashes. Long, pretty eyelashes, he had to admit.
He also had to admit that watching her get
ready for bed was going to be most . . . interesting. A tough job but, as they say, somebody's
gotta do it.

After putting the last pile of underwear on a
shelf in the armoire, she took out a black negligee and held it up. He could practically see
right through it. She tossed the negligee onto
the bed and put her hands to the top button on
her dress.

"Yes!" he shouted. "All right, babe! God, but
I'd forgotten how much I love the spy business. I
love this job!"

But she stopped. Something out of his view
caught her eye and she walked over to it.

"Come back to me, ba-a-a-by!" George cried.
He took a sip of his beer.

She stepped back into view holding a big
straw hat. It had a wide brim and a round
crown, with a little sprig of flowers on one side.
She tugged at the brim, as if trying to straighten
it, and frowned.

Her boyfriend took the hat from her and
tugged a bit himself, then handed it back as he
went to a suitcase and took out a bottle of wine.

Wine? A hat? What was this, some kinky sex
thing? He sat up straighter in the bed, even
more interested.

Paavo put the wine bottle on the bureau and
the hat on top of it. A hat rack. That's all it was.
He sank down again.

She shook her head, looking around the room, then glanced up. He nearly dropped his beer. She was staring straight at him. She pointed.

She'd seen the phony smoke detector! He should have known he couldn't fool the Hydra with a dumb trick like that. Now she was on to him.

But a second later, Paavo picked up the hat and makeshift hat rack and he, too, peered at the top of the armoire. What was going on? George wondered.

Then Paavo walked toward the camera. With each step a sinking feeling hit the pit of George's stomach.

"No!" He jumped off the bed. "Stop! Not up there!"

But despite his shrieks, Paavo reached up to the top of the armoire.

George now watched a perfectly focused picture of the Hydra's straw hat. And that was all.

27

In the center of the Hotel del Sud nestled a small open-air courtyard. There, the hotel staff served a simple continental breakfast of coffee, Mexican-style cinnamon-flavored hot chocolate, a variety of sweet buns, and *churros*.

As Angie stepped into the courtyard for breakfast, she stopped dead in her tracks, causing Paavo to bump into her. Seated in the courtyard were the four people they had met at the restaurant last evening. The Duchievors and George Gresham sat at one table, and Shawn MacDougall at another. All were having breakfast and reading English-language newspapers.

Angie and Paavo said good morning to them, then sat off by themselves.

"Hello there," Livingstone said, coming up behind them with a cup of coffee. "I believe I saw you both in a nearby restaurant last night. May I share your table?"

Angie jumped at the sound of his voice. For a big man, he was amazingly light-footed. Now he was playacting. What next?

"Please do," Paavo said, indicating an empty chair.

"Good morning," Angie said, nervously looking around. Not sure what to say, she finally blurted out, "You sound English."

Livingstone sat down at their table.

Just then, a large Mexican woman, age fifty or so, her black hair combed straight back into a traditional bun, walked into the courtyard carrying glasses and a pitcher of cold, freshly squeezed orange juice. She put the tray on the table where Shawn MacDougall sat alone. "Do you mind, *señor*?" she asked, loud enough that Angie overheard her.

"Not at all," he said, half standing to give a slight bow before he sat down again.

"I am Juanita," she said. "I have noticed you sitting here alone each morning, so I said to myself, today I will talk to him." Her gaze caught his and she smiled. He blushed, glancing around to see if anyone had noticed. Angie pretended she hadn't.

"You, *señor*," the woman went on as she filled glasses with juice, "should have two glasses. You are much too thin. Does your wife not feed you?"

"I have no wife," he said.

"Then I must take care to feed you well," she said. With that she smiled, winked, and began handing out glasses of orange juice to each person at the tables. Angie noticed a decided swish to her step that hadn't been there when she first walked into the courtyard.

Angie and Paavo glanced at each other and grinned.

Livingstone cleared his throat and bent close. "I think both of you should begin your sightseeing very soon. I'll watch your room."

"Who are those people?" Paavo asked, indicating with his eyes the four he spoke of.

"I don't know," Livingstone admitted. "Whoever they are, don't worry about them. They have nothing to do with us."

"They were awfully curious last night for people who have nothing to do with us," Angie said.

"I doubt you need to worry. I'll see what the hotel owner knows. I shouldn't be concerned if I were you."

"If you say so," Angie said dubiously.

Paavo didn't reply.

"We'll meet in the lobby at nine tonight," Livingstone said, "and I'll let you know how it went."

"Nine it is." Paavo stood, as did Angie. "We'll see you then. And be careful."

Livingstone's eyes narrowed. "You're not my keeper, my good man. I'll be careful. But whatever happens, happens."

Paavo frowned as Livingstone gave him a slight nod, then sat back and watched them leave.

*   *   *

"Did you see that?" George whispered to the others.

Shawn MacDougall joined them.

"Ve saw," Grundil said. "But vat does it mean?"

"The big Englishman was sitting at an outside table at the restaurant last night," MacDougall said. "They acted like they didn't know each other, and now they're having breakfast together."

"So vhat? Ve ate dinner together, but this morning ve didn't eat breakfast vith them," Béla said.

"That's true." MacDougall frowned, trying to reflect on the meaning of it all.

"This is the piece I needed," George announced. "The evidence that proves how sneaky and deceitful the woman is. Now I'm more sure than ever that what I suspected last night is, in fact, true!"

"Do tell us, dahling," Grundil said. "All night you looked like the cat who svallowed the canary. I really can't take it much longer."

George leaned closer to the center of the table. So did the others. He looked over each shoulder to make sure no one was nearby and listening. Again, so did the others. Then he lowered his voice and said, "That woman is the Hydra!"

"No!" Béla and Grundil cried.

"The what?" MacDougall asked.

"Von of the bad guys," Grundil explained. MacDougall's eyes widened.

"But she doesn't look or act like somevon who can elude people, or steal secrets, or kill anyvon," Béla said. "She seems very nice."

George clenched his fists. "That's what makes her so good at her work. Don't you see? She fools everyone. But not us. Now that we know—"

"Vait! Vhat proof do you have?" Grundil asked.

"Too much to go into, but last night she immediately found a minicamera I'd planted in her room and disengaged it. She's that good!"

The others showed by their stunned expressions just how impressed they were.

"Today, we'll have to follow them and see what they're up to, see if the colonel makes any connection with them," George said. "I'll watch the colonel. Grundil, you watch the woman. MacDougall, take the man, and Béla, er, you can watch the hotel."

"Or perhaps I vill take the man and Mac-Dougall the voman," Grundil said. "They say the Hydra does not vork alone. Her companion appears to be the more dangerous of the two, in my opinion, and ve should plan accordingly." She gave MacDougall a pointed stare.

He cleared his throat. "The man is very big. I think Grundil is right."

"Vhat about the older, fat man?" Grundil asked. "Shouldn't somevon vatch him?"

"A waste of time," George said dismissively. "Look at him. He's nothing."

Grundil shrugged. "Myself, I vould have somevon vatch him, but I've got the young, handsome von, so I'm sure I'll have my hands full."

"We all will," George said. "All of you, go to your respective posts, and we'll rendezvous at nineteen hundred hours." He checked his watch, stood up, and said, "Now go!"

Grundil watched as the three men jumped up and dashed from the courtyard. She shook her head and poured herself another cup of coffee.

28

Colonel Ortega wandered into the breakfast room wearing only pajama bottoms and smoking a cigar. His hair was a mass of disheveled spikes, and it was clear from his bloodshot eyes and the greenish cast to his skin that he'd had a few too many last evening while waiting for the Hydra to contact him.

"Did you hear from her this morning?" he immediately demanded.

Eduardo Catalán was reading the morning newspaper and breakfasting on a baguette, strong black coffee, and orange juice, a carryover from the days when he lived in Paris. He slowly folded the paper, creasing it neatly with one finger, and put it at the side of his coffee cup.

"I have heard nothing, my colonel," he said.

"Damn her!" The colonel sank heavily into a nearby chair. Immediately his housekeeper was at his side, quietly pouring him coffee and putting an ashtray by the cup. "She has had a day to contact me. Maybe it is time for me to go on board the ship and find out what this game is that she is playing. Whatever it is, I do not like it."

"Give her time," Eduardo said. "She would not pull a fast one on you. Whatever is wrong, I am sure she will fix it."

"But it has got to be serious or she would not be doing this when she knows I am waiting for a signal."

"I know," Eduardo cautioned. "That in itself is reason not to go onto the ship, or in any way draw attention to ourselves, until we know exactly what we are up against."

"Hmpf." The colonel took the newspaper from Eduardo's side and opened it up. "I do not like waiting on the whims of a woman!"

"What if we simply stay on the ship?" Mike Jones suggested. "And when it leaves, we do, too. Let's just forget about the colonel and his formula. Let him find the damn thing."

"I can't do that," the Hydra said. She lifted one of the heavy knives from the butcher block storage rack on the counter and tested its sharpness with her thumb. "My reputation would be ruined. In this business, you're only as successful as your last case. Anyway, on the off chance the professor's death is traced to Ortega in some way, I need to make sure he doesn't talk to the authorities about me."

"About you? Why would he? He ordered the hit—he's behind the whole thing."

"With a man like Ortega, one needs hard evidence. Receiving the formula will involve him enough that he won't be inclined to cooperate with the authorities. If I don't give him the formula, there's the chance he'd point the authorities in my direction. He'd have no reason not to. And I'd have no proof against him."

"Can he identify you?" Jones asked.

"He might. I met with him in person in Rio. I wore a blond wig, a mole on my chin—a kind of Marilyn Monroe vamp look that turns men Ortega's age especially hot. But it might not have been enough.

"I couldn't go too far because I needed to convince him that I was the one for the job. That he could trust me to take the formula to him, and that the *Valhalla* was the perfect way to get it out of the country without anyone knowing."

"Well, I guess you were almost right," Jones said.

Her hand tightened on the knife handle. "I was absolutely right. It would have gone off without a hitch if Ingerson hadn't gotten sick!"

"Maybe he was holding it back from you on purpose."

"Shut up! He wouldn't dare! I can't help but think the cause of my trouble has to do with the passengers. One of them—or maybe more than one—wasn't what he, or she, seemed."

"You're right," Jones said softly, his gaze never leaving the knife in her hand.

"We can still pull this off, damn it!" She slammed the tip of the knife deep into the chopping block. Jones flinched. "We've gone through the ship, through all the cabins. The Amalfi woman has to have it on her. There's no other explanation. So we steal her purse, and if we can't find it in there, we steal her."

"You mean kidnap her?"

She slid her fingers under the waistband of his jeans, taking hold of his belt and jerking him close, almost eye to eye. "I don't give a damn if we have to slice her into little pieces to find that formula. One way or another, we're going to get it." Then she shoved him away from her and left the room.

29

Angie took a pamphlet about Mazatlán from a table by the front desk of the hotel. It was old and yellowed. Obviously this wasn't a hotel that catered to tourists, but since her interests lay in the historical parts of town, which wouldn't have changed, it didn't matter. She and Paavo had a whole day to play tourist.

Paavo had talked her into leaving her big tote bag in the room. He remembered her complaining about Mike Jones's concern about it. Maybe it meant nothing. On the other hand, he wasn't leaving anything to chance, and if Mike Jones was a part of this—and Paavo suspected he was—Jones could take the bag. Instead of carrying a purse, he had persuaded her to strap around her waist a pouch like bicyclists and other athletic types wore.

Normally, she hated wearing waist packs. She felt like a kangaroo having a pouch stuck on her stomach. Besides, it was so small she could carry only essentials: her passport, credit cards, lipstick, compact, comb, money, and keys. When she tossed in a tube of mascara, just in case, it bulged more unflatteringly than ever.

She was so focused on the bulge around her middle that she made no protest when Paavo convinced her to leave her camera behind, too.

Pamphlet in hand, they set out for the Basilica de la Inmaculada Concepción, to be followed by the Plaza Republicana, and finally the big central market.

Livingstone almost missed seeing Mike Jones slip into Angie and Paavo's room, he did it so quickly. The Englishman had been standing behind the door of his own room, peering through a glass he'd installed the day before in place of the normal peephole. Now, instead of affording a view of whoever might be knocking at his door, it gave a wide-angle panorama of the hallway, and an especially good view of the entrance to the room opposite.

As a backup, Livingstone had put a bug in the Smith-Amalfi room, in case someone entered while he wasn't looking through the peephole, which was one of the more boring ways to spend one's time.

This stakeout had certainly turned out to be a lot easier than most. It hadn't lasted even an hour when, already, he was about to catch his man. Instinctively, he patted the gun in his jacket pocket.

He'd wait five minutes, then go in. By that time, Jones should be smack in the middle of whatever criminal activity he had in mind.

Livingstone put on his earphones to listen to what was going on in the room. He hadn't mentioned to Paavo that he'd bugged their room, but he was sure the cop would understand. Besides, Livingstone had done it once before—in their cabin on the ship. Unfortunately, it'd been found before he'd managed to learn anything. Now he heard the opening of a drawer. Still searching . . . just as he'd suspected.

Suddenly something hard and cold pressed against the back of his neck, right at the base of his skull, a most deadly spot for a bullet to be placed.

A sick feeling oozed through him. Moving only his eyes, he caught a reflection of the room in the mirror over the dresser . . . of the open balcony door . . . of the face of his assailant.

"You!" he cried.

The silencer caused the bullet to go off with only a dull popping sound, a bizarre prelude to the roar it made when it entered his skull.

Mazatlán was much larger and busier than Angie had expected, and with fewer historical tourist attractions. Even the big basilica, which had a lovely gilded altar, had been built in the late nineteenth century. Very little architecture from the early Spanish settlement survived.

After checking out the central market, she and Paavo walked to the beach, the Playa Olas Altas. There she quickly discovered that the stores she was most interested in were in the new, northern part of the city, the Zona Dorada, or Golden Zone.

They caught a taxi. Looking into the side-view mirror, Paavo saw that Grundil Duchievor and the strangely named Shawn MacDougall had also caught one and were doggedly following them to the Golden Zone. Once in the Zone, the odd couple got out of their cab about a half block down the street from Paavo and Angie.

As Angie began her study of the boutiques of Mazatlán, Grundil and MacDougall kept their distance, sometimes following her into the larger shops or waiting outside as she went into the smaller ones. Paavo finally concluded that they were simply watching Angie's every move and were most likely harmless.

"Oh!" Angie cried. "This store is having a huge sale. Let's check it out."

Paavo stepped into yet another store with her. It was bigger than any of the others they'd been in so far, filled with many rows of dresses, all being pawed over by masses of women. Overwhelmed by the sudden noise of the shoppers, the clatter of cash registers, the ringing of telephones, and the wildly hued displays of clothes in clashing plaids and stripes and dots, he backed up. This was worse than chasing criminals. "I don't think so."

"Come on," she urged. "It'll take me only a minute or two."

He shook his head. "I'll be sitting at a table at that outdoor café across the street. When you're through here, come and join me."

"That's fine," she said, handing him her shopping bags. "Would you mind holding these for me? I need a nice dress to wear when we go to dinner this evening. We should try one of the restaurants facing the beach."

Clutching Angie's shopping bags, Paavo fled the store before she could even say good-bye.

Although it was true that the shopping was giving him a definite hatred of crowds—a condition he had never known he had until he accompanied Angie on a couple of her shopping sprees—what he really wanted to do was call Yosh.

"Looks like you're with a very dull group of people," Yosh said as soon as Paavo got him on the line.

"Tell me about it."

"Ruby and Harold Cockburn, retired military and retired statistician for the Department of Education—looks like she made sergeant. Nellie and Marvin Nebler, housewife and retired used-car salesman."

"What about the last guy?" Paavo asked.

"At least he's more interesting. He's supposed to be some sort of art dealer, but everything about him is vague. It's all there—the papers say the right thing, but it's too plastic, too pat, if you know what I mean. Just a hunch."

"Okay. That's good. And Ingerson, the steward?"

"Botulism. He died yesterday. Kidney and liver failure."

"Botulism? How the hell . . . ?" He hadn't been expecting to hear anything like that. Poison, yes, but not botulism that was so erratic it wasn't used by killers. Only nature dealt blows like botulism. "What about the cook?"

"Peter Lichty had some sort of nervous breakdown. He kept muttering about a woman. That's all anyone could tell me. INS saw to it that he was sent back to Norway. He had no papers to allow him to stay."

"A woman. Interesting," Paavo murmured.

"Your last question," Yosh said, "about Professor Von Mueller. It's a big case, Paav, and a lid's been clamped on it. I had to call in some big-time favors."

"It's appreciated."

"The guy was murdered. It's not in the papers, but he was. A couple of homicide cops in Berkeley were doing a routine investigation—being careful, of course, because it's not every day that you investigate the murder of some scientist—when all of a sudden, the FBI shows up. Everyone involved is more nervous than a long-tailed cat in a room full of rocking chairs, as they say."

"What's going on?" Paavo asked impatiently.

"Didn't I just say there was a lid on it?" Yosh loved to torment his serious partner. His partner wasn't laughing, though. "Okay, here goes. The glorious, albeit dead, Professor Von Mueller is said to have invented a way to create cold fusion, which is a way to create nuclear energy."

"Nuclear energy?" That was the last thing he'd expected to hear.

"Yes, but with a difference. A big difference. There's no heat, no core that could melt down and cause another Chernobyl—in fact, there's not even any nuclear waste to store for the next gazillion years."

Yosh's words caught Paavo's interest. "Is this for real? Safe nuclear energy?"

"Well, that's the problem. No one knows if cold fusion can really occur or if it's just a theory. The Berkeley PD didn't understand what the scientists were talking about and tried to cut off access to the lab to protect the crime scene. Then the FBI brought in some of their own scientists. They spent a day in there going through the professor's files and computer. Then the FBI took the professor's computer, his disks, and all his records. The Berkeley PD heard them say that it was looking real good, but all they could find was old information. They were missing the actual formula and all the most recent data that led up to it."

Yosh chuckled. "I should add that the crime scene was a complete mess. Based on finger-prints and other evidence at the scene, the BPD had incontrovertible proof that six different FBI agents and three scientists killed Von Mueller."

"What a nightmare!" The homicide inspector in Paavo shuddered at the thought of having the crime scene wrecked that way. "So, where was the actual formula? Was it stolen? Is that what they think was behind his murder?"

"The reason the FBI got involved in the first place was that there were rumors the professor had sold the formula to some international consortium instead of keeping it here in the good ol' USA. The trouble is, it wasn't his to sell. He developed it, but he did it as an employee of the university and on government grants. There was no way he could argue he came up with it in his home office in the evening. He had to do most of the work at the Lawrence Laboratory, and it is specifically what the government paid him to come up with."

"Interesting. What else did you learn?"

"I think that's about it. Except that the going price for the formula to create cold fusion is around a hundred million dollars. And that's not from the people who want to use it—it's from the oil and gas industries that would be hurt by a new, cheap source of energy. They want to see it buried."

Paavo whistled. "Anyone check the professor's bank account?"

"Swiss bank account, you mean? As far as I know, the Berkeley PD didn't have the money for any long-distance calls."

"I'm not surprised. Speaking of money, I'd better get off the phone. This will cost a small fortune."

"You're right, buddy. And after you get off the phone, see what you can do about getting away from that ship. Between botulism, phony art dealers, and people asking about cold fusion formulas, it's not the best place for a vacation."

"You're right."

"But at the same time . . ." Yosh stopped, hesitant.

"Yes?" Paavo asked.

"Keep investigating. You sound like my partner again."

Actually, Angie had to admit, she was glad he'd left her alone for a short while. What she wanted to do even more than look at dresses was to buy something for him. Although this vacation hadn't turned out the way it was supposed to, she felt closer to him somehow—ever since he'd told her on the ship how much he'd been bothered by the death of the police officer. It also helped clarify her own feelings about his job. He was a cop—that defined his nature, his personality. And she didn't want those things to change.

Now, what could she buy him? She turned down an aisle between some dresses. She'd found in the past that at times, when she was mindlessly shopping for herself, she'd come up with ideas for other things—like a gift for her man.

*   *   *

Shawn MacDougall couldn't believe the woman had disappeared. He'd noticed her abandon her companion and then begin to drift among the clothes as if she hadn't a care in the world. While most shoppers were pulling dresses, suits, and blouses off the racks and holding them up against themselves, she was walking up one aisle and down the next, pretending to be deep in thought. How deeply could one think about little black dresses and sequin-studded evening shoes? He hadn't dared to get too close, of course, but had simply followed behind to see what she was up to. Then, somehow, he'd lost her.

A number of women were giving him strange glances, as if they thought he was a masher, or maybe a cross-dresser. He even told one he was looking for a present for his wife.

He shouldn't have let Grundil talk him into watching the woman. It was too embarrassing. On the other hand, what was his alternative? The man? No way! Too big and tough-looking.

Then again, the woman was the Hydra—tougher than any man, he'd heard.

He squared his narrow shoulders. He had studied Greek mythology. The Hydra was a ferocious, multiheaded monster that only Hercules could kill. Well, if Hercules could manage it, so could he. He threw out his chest and charged into the racks of velvet pantsuits where he'd last sighted the Hydra.

Still, he couldn't shake the thought of her callous, calculating brown eyes. The eyes of a killer. Her companion, he now realized, was clearly just a dupe. Blue-eyed, big, and brain-dead. Obviously, she just kept him around to watch her back by day, and he didn't want to think about what the big moose watched by night.

No wonder Grundil had selected the man for herself. She'd pulled what George would have called "a fast one" on him. Took the easier of the two. Could he blame her?

He cautiously backed up and worked his way past a row of strapless evening gowns. Where had the Hydra disappeared to? Could she have noticed him following her? He didn't think so, but she was pretty sharp. Could she be watching, ready to pounce? He'd heard how cold-blooded she was.

At least he had his lethal weapons with him—a stiletto knife up his sleeve, a palm-size pistol in his pocket, a poisoned pin in the lining of his belt, and, most important of all, his hands. He knew tae kwon do, and there were several deadly blows that could take out a man three times his size. That little woman, even smaller than his five feet four inches, would be no problem for him at all.

He buried himself deep among the satin negligees and, holding his hands out in front of him, assumed the ready position. Of course, everyone knew the story of how the Hydra had once sneaked up on three men while they were guarding diamonds and killed them with her bare hands.

He wasn't afraid of her, though. She wouldn't kill him in this store with all these people as witnesses! Unless, of course, she made it look like an accident . . .

If she did kill him, he wondered how long it'd be before anyone realized he was gone. To the other spies at the hotel, he was no more than an afterthought. No one thought much of him, he was sure. His family had disowned him when he decided to work for the government. Now that the government no longer wanted him, they were even more disrespectful.

He wondered if they'd care when they heard he was dead, killed by some Western female. His ancestors would be most displeased. Of course, he reminded himself, the government wisely preached that he need not worry about ancestors any longer. The state was right. Only what the state thought mattered.

And sometimes his mother.

His breathing quickened. Maybe he should forget about the Hydra and just go back to the hotel. He didn't know exactly why he was following her, anyway. Why not give up on this spy stuff and build himself a new life? Maybe get to know Juanita Cruz better. She was always nice to him at breakfast. This morning she'd even spoken to him.

Having come to a decision, he felt better. He began to tiptoe backward with great delibera-

tion, concealing his progress under a filmy camouflage of pink nightgowns. His retreat took
him directly toward a rack of see-through ted-
dies. Suddenly, he heard the sound of clothes
hangers being parted. He felt a breeze hit the
back of his neck. Then he heard a voice cry out,
"What a surprise!"

He recognized that voice. Sweat beaded on
his furrowed forehead, and his Adam's apple
began working furiously. Slowly, with his head
bowed—more because he was afraid to look up
than because he was being respectful—he
turned. Through blurred vision he saw something purple and chunky on the ground. He
blinked and saw that it was a shoe, the toe of a
fashionable woman's shoe. There was a foot in
the shoe, and it was attached to a leg. His heart
raced; involuntary gulping accompanied the
fluttering of his Adam's apple. He forced himself to raise his eyes past the purple and white
striped dress, past the silver necklace, past the
pointed chin, full lips, small nose . . .

Big brown eyes, large and devouring, stared
directly at him. He was looking at the Hydra!

The little man's scream rang out through the
store, causing everyone nearby to turn and stare.

Rubbing her ringing ears, Angie saw the
man's eyes turn into huge circles. His hands
began to chop the air wildly, and strange *"hup,
hup"* sounds came from his throat.

His Adam's apple bobbed so fast that his bow

tie unraveled. Backpedaling furiously, he seemed unaware of the danger he was heading toward. "Stop!" she cried.

But that only seemed to make his legs move even faster. Back he went, arms hacking, feet bounding higher with each step, until, to Angie's complete amazement, he backed into a display of bikini panties. Reaching out to the top of the rack to catch himself, he pulled the whole thing down with him. Panties and rack landed in a heap on the man, who lay smothered in lace and nylon, peering out through the leg hole of a little French-cut number adorned with ribbons and rosettes.

As a flock of salesclerks tried to free him, Angie quietly made her way to the door, then ran across the street to find Paavo.

They were drinking coffee at an outdoor café when they saw an ambulance pull up in front of the dress shop. Angie had told Paavo about her strange encounter with Shawn MacDougall, and he'd told her the information he'd received from Yoshiwara. Minutes later, paramedics emerged pushing Shawn MacDougall in a wheelchair. But when they reached the truck, he suddenly jumped up and, with a pronounced limp, ran down the street.

The paramedics shrugged, got back into the ambulance, and drove away.

"Why was he following me?" Angie wondered aloud.

"We'll find out what Livingstone knows when we see him tonight. He said he'll check on Mac-Dougall and the others," Paavo reminded her. "We need to find out if they're dangerous or not." He glanced at Angie and chuckled. "Although from what you tell me about Mac-Dougall, it sounds like he was a lot more afraid of you than you were of him."

Angie began to giggle, and she held the napkin to her lips. "You should have seen him with those frilly panties draped over his ear," she said, gasping for air as the giggles became a full-fledged laugh.

Paavo joined her.

30

The colonel put down the telephone receiver. "She found it. She says she will have it here tonight."

"Do you believe her?" Eduardo asked, looking up from the *Times* of London. They were seated in Ortega's game room.

"Why shouldn't I?"

"It seems to me she's stalling. What if she has found out just how valuable the formula is and is trying to find someone else to sell it to?"

"She wouldn't dare!" Ortega bellowed.

"You did, my colonel," Eduardo replied.

Ortega's eyes narrowed. "What are you saying?"

"You were going to give the formula to the consortium, but instead you decided to sell it to the highest bidder on your own," he stated logically.

"But it will be *mine* to sell," Ortega yelled.

"Paid for with the consortium's money," Eduardo pointed out.

"You object, *amigo*?" The colonel's words were menacing.

"Of course not," Eduardo replied. "They owe you that money—and more."

"That is how I feel," Ortega agreed.

"As soon as she shows up with the formula," Eduardo said, "it is yours to do with as you wish. *If* she shows up with it."

"She has no choice." Ortega rubbed his chin. "But perhaps you are right, and we should not wait. I will demand she give it to me immediately."

"And if she does not?"

Ortega's eyes were hard. "No one refuses me."

31

By ten o'clock, Paavo was worried. Livingstone was an hour late. That meant trouble. Livingstone had struck him as a man who didn't
miss appointments unless something was seri-
ously wrong.

After the dress shop incident, Paavo and
Angie had gone to a restaurant called Tres Islas
for a meal of *parrillada de mariscos,* a mixed
seafood grill featuring shrimp, oyster, crab, and
swordfish. They'd returned to the hotel a little
before nine.

Paavo had knocked on the door to Livingstone's room a couple of times but received no
answer. Their own room had been searched,
and Angie's tote bag was missing. Paavo wasn't
sure what to make of it. Had Livingstone caught
the intruder? He should have, but without Livingstone's okay, Paavo didn't want to assume
anything was safe.

The hotel owner hadn't heard from or seen Livingstone all day.

While Paavo waited in the lobby, Angie decided to check out the courtyard of the hotel. She walked down the noisy tiled hallway and was almost at the French doors when she heard footsteps behind her. George Gresham was heading her way. She didn't want to talk to him and hurried on a little way, then ducked into an open door. She found herself in a corridor that led to the hotel's laundry and small kitchen facilities. She stepped into the shadows where she couldn't readily be seen. Voices came from the kitchen. Moving farther along the wall, she slipped into a recessed area near the pantry door and watched.

"My big *mamacita*," Shawn MacDougall said, throwing his arms as far as he could around the waist of the woman who had served orange juice that morning.

"My little China doll," Juanita responded, bending over and crushing the seated Shawn to her ample breasts. "I'm so sorry you were hurt today."

"But I am so glad it brought me to you," he said, his voice muffled. She patted his leg, which was propped up on another chair, cushioned with a pillow.

Since the two had eyes only for each other, Angie figured she'd quietly leave as soon as she thought George Gresham was out of the way. But no such luck.

"So here you are, MacDougall," Gresham bellowed as he marched down the corridor to the kitchen, right past Angie, who was still lurking against the wall by the pantry. "Have you seen the Hydra?" he asked. "I thought I saw her headed out to the courtyard, but she wasn't there."

The Hydra? Angie thought. That was the woman Livingstone had mentioned. Was she here, too? Could Grundil be the Hydra? She looked the way a Hydra might look. But she'd seen Grundil going up to her room about a half hour ago.

On the other hand, George might have caught a glimpse of *her*, she thought, when she was in the hallway. But he couldn't possibly think she . . . No, he couldn't think *that*.

MacDougall pried himself free from Juanita. "I didn't see her. I was just having a cup of tea."

Gresham eyed the woman. "Ri-i-i-i-ght."

"*Señora* Cruz and I have been talking," Mac-Dougall said. "She is recently widowed, I'm sorry to say."

"Not so recent," Juanita said, beaming at Shawn. "But you're sweet, *Señor* MacDougall." She glanced at Gresham. "He's so thoughtful."

"Thoughtful or not, he's got work to do," Gresham said sternly. "We've got a Hydra to catch. Let's go, MacDougall. You're a part of this team."

George strode out of the kitchen, Mac-Dougall limping behind him, and Juanita bustling after them both, chastising George for making her poor, sick, sweet *querido* go with him.

Angie waited until the coast was clear, then went in search of Paavo. Now she had even more to tell him about the mysterious Hydra.

The result was not what she'd planned.

"You're going to the airport," Paavo announced with a glint in his eyes that she was all too familiar with.

"You mean *we're* going to the airport," Angie said firmly. Did he really think he could send her to Acapulco without him?

"I'll fly out later, after I pack up our belongings. But first I want you out of Mazatlán as soon as possible, and I don't want you anywhere near our luggage."

"Now wait a minute—"

"It'll be safer if I don't have to worry about you, okay?"

She'd heard that argument before. One time too many, in fact. She was tired of his wanting to scuttle her off to somewhere safe while he put himself in danger. "And just what am I supposed to do? Go sightseeing in Acapulco without you?"

"We don't know what's happened to Livingstone. I think he'd have called if everything was settled. I don't like it—especially if people are thinking you're this Hydra creature. So Acapulco is out. I want you back in San Francisco."

That was too much. "Now, wait—"

"Angie, it's not safe." His jaw was stubborn.

She knew that look. "I listened to Livingstone against my better judgment. What he said made sense at the time, but now I don't know. I've got a feeling things might have turned ugly."

"You don't know that for sure!" she argued.

"Let's go, right now," he said.

"Without you? No."

"No? You've got to."

"No! You said the other day to Livingstone that I shouldn't be endangered because I'm a civilian. Well, let me remind you that in a couple of weeks you'll be a civilian, too. And right now you're on vacation."

"That has nothing to do with it," he said.

"It has everything to do with it. This isn't your responsibility. You've decided to give that up, remember?"

He frowned. "Angie—"

"You're right, too, not to worry about finding another job," she quickly added. "You'll find one easily. In fact, I'm sure my father can get you a great one in his shoe business. Not sales—something better. Maybe in bookkeeping. You'll easily double your salary. Won't it be great?"

"I know what you're doing, Angie. You're not exactly subtle, you know."

"You see it as a bad joke, don't you? Doesn't that tell you something about yourself, Inspector Smith? About who you are and what you are?"

He shut his eyes a moment. "I just don't know."

"If you truly wanted to quit the force, you'd fly out of here with me, right now. Think about it."

"Hell," he said, then took her arm and rushed her through the lobby to the street.

She had to practically run to keep up with his long-legged stride. He kept a tight grip on her, frowning mightily.

"Are you leaving with me?" she asked.

"No."

"Why not?"

"Forget it."

"At least tell me why you're being so secretive," she asked between panted breaths.

He stopped a moment and looked at her. "Do you honestly think Livingstone would leave us waiting here if he were able to reach us and tell us what's going on?"

"Well, no, but—"

"Something's happened to him. And if it's happened to him, it could happen to us. I want you out of here. I'll be right behind you," he added, almost as an afterthought.

"You will?" she asked.

He nodded.

That took her aback. He truly must be worried. "We definitely need to go back to San Francisco, then?"

"What choice do we have?" he asked. "We don't know enough about what's going on, except that it's international and it's big. We'll contact Interpol once we're home."

She glanced up at his intense blue eyes and watched them surveying doorways, parked cars, and the few vehicles that drove past them as they hurried through the dark, quiet streets. She had to admit he was right. As the evening had dragged on, and especially after listening to George's strange words in the kitchen, she'd grown increasingly uneasy.

The Hydra, she thought. First on the ship, then here in Mazatlán. Who in the world was she?

"If there are no direct flights back to San Francisco soon, get on one to Los Angeles," Paavo said. He pushed her into a doorway and stood in front of her, peering up and down both sides of the street to see if anyone was following them. "I don't want you sitting around the airport any longer than absolutely necessary. I don't know what these people want with you, or why, and I don't want *you* to find out."

"I thought you said you were coming with me," she said.

"I will, quite soon. But don't hang around the airport waiting for me. Take the first flight out, and I'll follow. To be certain there's no danger, don't even go to your apartment. Go to your parents' place. I'll meet you there tomorrow."

"I don't get it. We can leave together. I'll go ahead and buy tickets for both of us."

"I don't want our stuff left behind."

She grabbed his shirtsleeve, wanting to shake sense into him. "Our stuff isn't important." She couldn't believe he'd stay behind just to pack. "Anyway, we can have the hotel ship it later, once we're home and safe."

He placed his hands on her shoulders, lightly stroking them. "It's important to me," he said softly.

She knew he wasn't telling her everything. She could have said that their belongings weren't that valuable—nothing compared to the chance of his being hurt. But he knew that. He wanted her out of the way, and away from him for now. He had promised to be right behind her. She had to hold on to that.

"Okay," she said finally. "But don't dawdle. I expect you to be no more than an hour behind me."

"Don't worry about me," he said, pulling her against his chest.

"I don't like this, Paavo." She wrapped her arms around him.

"Come on," he said, gently releasing himself from her embrace. "Let's find a cab to take you to the airport."

They hurried down another couple of side streets, then to a main boulevard, where they hailed a taxi.

Paavo gave the cab driver orders to take Angie to the airport, then waited, hoping that he wouldn't see anyone following her cab. He didn't. She was safely on her way.

He headed back to the hotel.

Angie walked through the quiet terminal, searching for the next flight to San Francisco or Los Angeles. Suddenly, she stopped in her tracks.

Paavo was going to look for Livingstone.

That was why he wanted her out of the way. He had said he was afraid something had happened to the man and that they might be next. But he wasn't about to remove himself from harm's way. He would try to find Livingstone first. To get him out of whatever danger he was in, if at all possible.

And to do it meant that he himself would be in danger.

The new Paavo—the one who insisted he was going to quit the force and act like any other civilian—wouldn't be going after Livingstone.

The old Paavo was back. At least as far as trying to help a fellow officer. But as much as she was glad he was back, she hated the danger he might be placing himself in.

She turned around and headed back toward the airport entrance, back toward the taxis returning to Mazatlán.

Should she go to the police? With what story? What evidence? The police in San Francisco wouldn't do anything in a situation like this— they'd tell her to file a missing-person report unless there was some real evidence that someone had been harmed. Even if there was such evidence, a missing person wasn't necessarily tops on their priority list, especially when the supposedly missing one was a secret agent with Interpol and the name they had for him probably wasn't legitimate. They wouldn't know how or where to begin. Or even if they should.

Would the police in Mazatlán react any differently? She didn't even have to ask the question.

Her step slowed as she reached the main entrance. Maybe she was overreacting and Paavo would quickly take care of a few things— maybe find Livingstone, in fact, and join her. She took a seat in a lounge area with a clear view of the entry doors. She'd watch for Paavo to come through them.

And if he didn't? She wondered if she could do as he'd requested, as she'd promised. Could she fly back to San Francisco without him?

32

Only a dim night-light was shining in the lobby of the Hotel del Sud when Paavo returned. He went to the house phone and called Livingstone's room. No answer.

He took the stairs two at a time up to the second floor, but instead of going into his own room he stopped at Livingstone's. On his key ring was a small pocketknife, and one of the implements on it was a steel toothpick. He couldn't imagine using it on his teeth, but he'd managed to open a door lock with it before. The locks in this hotel were simple. He looked from the lock to the key ring and back again.

Livingstone had been sure there was no serious danger here. He'd been sure he'd carefully worked out his plan of action and didn't even need a backup. Livingstone was a pro—an international pro with years of experience. Everything was fine. Paavo told himself he was simply overreacting to a perceived danger, and that this was fallout from his experience with Ed Gillespie.

In about three minutes the door swung open and he walked into Livingstone's room.

The first thing he noticed was the smell. Not of death, but of blood. He took out his gun. He'd begun carrying it since they'd arrived in Mazatlán. Legal or not, he didn't care. The wallpaper had a smear on it, a rust-colored smear, as if someone had hastily tried, and failed, to wipe it clean. And the dark wooden floor right by the door, when he bent down and touched it, felt strangely slick.

Livingstone's suitcase was on the floor, and a few of his belongings were on the dresser and the nightstand by his bed.

He pulled open the closet door. The closet was empty except for a couple of shirts.

He walked into the bathroom. The smell of blood was stronger, more oppressive. An electric shaver and aftershave were by the sink. A toothbrush.

The shower curtain was pulled shut. With one hand clutching his gun, he reached out with the other, grabbed the curtain, and flung it aside.

His stomach turned. He jerked the curtain shut again, even though from a procedural view, it was a waste of time and effort. He was a homicide cop, and he'd seen all kinds of horror. But when half of a man's face has been torn away, even hardened cops find it hard to take.

He backed up, taking several deep breaths to clear his head. More than ever now, he needed his training to kick in, in order to find the person who had done this. It was time to bring the police into this whole ugly mess.

He opened the door to the hallway and froze.

The door to his and Angie's room was open, the lights on. A big man wearing a military uniform sat on a chair, three other men behind him. Paavo saw Mike Jones there, his hands awkwardly behind his back, as if they'd been tied. And in the doorway, looking straight at him across the hall, was a woman. A woman who looked strangely familiar.

"Won't you come and join us, Inspector Smith?" she said, her voice low. Why hadn't he recognized it as a woman's voice before? "We've been waiting for you."

By eight o'clock the next morning Paavo still hadn't arrived at the airport. He'd had all night to find Livingstone, pick up his luggage, and get away from the hotel. If he hadn't been able to handle it by then, it was probably because he couldn't.

Angie shivered to think of what that meant. But maybe she was letting her imagination run away with her and everything was fine. Livingstone had insisted that the thieves, or whatever they were, were only after their luggage and that no one would be harmed. She hoped he still felt that way.

Periodically, throughout the night, she'd left her seat in the passenger lounge to check with the airlines flying to L.A. or San Francisco to see if Paavo had caught a different flight or made reservations, on the off chance that she'd somehow missed him when he entered the airport.

But he hadn't, which meant he was still in Mazatlán.

By nine in the morning, she couldn't stand it any longer. She phoned the hotel and asked to speak to Paavo. The clerk came back on the line telling her there was no answer in Mr. Smith's room.

She caught a cab back to the hotel.

As the cab entered Avenida Olas Altas, she began to have second thoughts. Maybe returning to the hotel wasn't the smartest thing she'd ever considered doing. Livingstone was supposed to be inside watching her room, and he'd disappeared. Paavo probably had gone in looking for Livingstone, and now she didn't know where he was. Should she chance it?

At the Plaza Republicana, across from the basilica, she asked the driver to stop. She paid him, then ran into the park to a spot behind a bush from which she could watch the hotel entrance. She doubted anyone at the hotel could see her peeking at it through the shrubbery.

If she saw Paavo or Livingstone arrive or leave, she could sprint across the park and reach them in no time.

But she sat on the bench, watching and waiting to no avail. Where were they?

"What do you think?" George Gresham and the other ex-spies stood in a semicircle, watching the Hydra stare at the hotel. They'd noticed her in the park as they were strolling back to the hotel from the central market, where they'd been arguing over what to do about the colonel and the Hydra—or if the situation was too big and too dangerous for them to take on.

"Should ve grab her?" Béla asked.

"For vhat, dahling?" Grundil said. "You can't just go about snatching people, even if you suspect they are dangerous."

"*Especially* if you suspect they are dangerous," MacDougall added nervously.

"We can get her for what she did to Mac-Dougall here," George said. "Look at his limp. She's a menace!"

MacDougall was using a cane this morning.

Grundil put her hands on her hips. "Don't take this as an insult, dahlings. I know you are all good spies. But frankly, I don't think she is any more the Hydra than I am." She paused for them to protest, but they said nothing, waiting for her to explain. "Look at her. Anyvon vith half a brain can see how scared she is. Vhere is her handsome boyfriend? That's the qvestion ve should be asking. I think ve should talk vith her. Find out vhat this is about."

"Where *is* her boyfriend?" MacDougall asked.

"Weren't you watching him, Grundil?"

"I vatched him sit in the lobby vith her until midnight. Then the two of them vent for a valk. Béla and I tried to follow, but they moved too fast for Béla to keep up vith. Ve debated vhat to do—should I go alone? Ve decided it vas easiest to go to a bar and vait for them to pass by again on their vay back to the hotel. But they didn't. Vhen it vas closing time, ve returned to the hotel and vent to bed."

"You know, Grundil, I'm getting a bit old for all this," Béla said. "Let us just forget it and open our restaurant." He turned to the others and continued, "I even have a name for it—A Taste of Transylvania, in honor of our home-land."

"Sounds yummy," George said with a smirk.

"He expects me to be the barmaid," Grundil said, glaring at her husband. "He has lost his marbles, as you vould say, George."

Béla shrugged.

"I repeat," Grundil announced, "ve need to go over there and talk vith her now. Find out vhat this is all about."

No one moved.

"Maybe just one of us should go," Mac-Dougall suggested. "I'd do it, but—" He motioned to his leg. "Obviously a man with an injury such as this . . ." He sighed.

"MacDougall's right," George said. "Just one should go. And I've already put myself in danger by scouting around in her room. What if she'd walked in on me? I'd have been dead meat!"

"I vould go," Grundil said. "But I know Béla vouldn't vant to put his vife in danger." She smiled sweetly at him, then pulled out a cigarette, walked over to a bench, sat down, and lit it.

"All right," Béla said with a sigh. "I'll go."

The little man walked toward Angie, coming up from behind her as she watched the hotel. He hoped she wasn't the sort who would shoot first and ask questions later. He'd heard Americans were big on that. He stopped and made lots of throat-clearing noises. No sense taking chances.

She turned. A flicker of caution appeared on her face, but as her gaze swept over him, he saw her relax. He knew he wasn't one to bring fear into any heart.

"Good morning," he said.

"Good morning," she replied.

"Are you alone?" he asked. "I don't see your friend."

"He'll be back soon." She was obviously lying.

"May I join you?" He pointed to the bench where she sat. She nodded. "So," he began, "how are you enjoying Mazatlán?"

"It could be better," she admitted soulfully.

"It isn't vhat you expected?" he said in a voice that as much as admitted he felt that way, too.

She glanced up at him, as if surprised. "To tell the truth," she said, "I hadn't thought about Mazatlán at all. We were headed for Acapulco."

"So, you vanted to vacation there?" Béla asked.

"Vacation, plus I had an assignment."

"Assignment?" The word had connotations that alarmed him—shades of *The Man From U.N.C.L.E.*, which had been popular all over Europe in his heyday. He'd always identified with Ilya.

"I had an assignment to write an article about dining out," Angie explained. "I'm a restaurant reviewer sometimes, and I planned to check out the best restaurants by night, and the beach by day, combining business with pleasure, so to speak."

Had she said what he thought she'd said? "You are a restaurant reviewer?" Overcome with relief, he laughed. "You know about cooking? Restaurants?"

"Yes," she said, puzzled by the amusement he seemed to find from that. "Somewhat."

"Oh, my good voman, you don't know vhat a surprise, and vhat a pleasure it is to hear that. You can't imagine vhat I first thought. Vell, enough of that already. To know vhat makes a fine restaurant . . . that is my dream, to own a restaurant of my own. I vould cook Romanian and Hungarian food. Of course, there isn't too much Romanian food that people in the Vest vould vant to eat, I'm afraid. Ve have a poor country, and ve eat vhatever ve can. Our best food is close to Hungarian cooking."

"Hungarian cuisine is wonderful," Angie said.

"I know it well. I'm particularly fond of foods like, let's see if I've got this right, *borgrácsgulyás?*"

"You know *borgrácsgulyás?*" Béla clapped his hands. "You *are* a cook!"

"Let's see," Angie said slowly, trying to remember, "beef, onions, potatoes—"

"Plus add beef heart to make it even better," he said.

"Really? I didn't know that. Okay, caraway—"

"Peppers and paprika."

"Lots of paprika, always, in a goulash."

"Just to speak of it makes my mouth vater," Béla cried. "So, vhy are you here instead of in Acapulco?"

Angie was frantic with worry over the strange goings-on around her, over not knowing where Paavo was or how to go about finding him. Ordinarily, under these circumstances, she would have been more wary. But somehow, this downcast yet friendly man who liked to cook appeared safe to talk to. Even if he couldn't help, he seemed like he'd at least offer sympathy.

"Someone seems to think I have something that I don't," she began. "And that person is apparently dangerous. It's a woman—and they call her the Hydra."

She watched Béla's eyes widen in alarm, but he said nothing.

She continued. "My friend and I were advised to stay here, but now I don't know where he is. He's"—it was harder to talk about this than she'd thought—"he's disappeared." Tears welled up. "I'm so worried about him, I don't know what to do!"

"Don't cry, please," Béla said. "Ve vill help you."

"I'm not crying." She dabbed at her tears. "I don't dare. I've got to keep an eye on the hotel. To look for Paavo."

"Vait here," Béla said, and hurried over to his friends. They huddled together; every so often one head would pop up and look at her. Soon all four of them trooped across the lawn and sat with her on the bench.

"Ve have decided you are not the Hydra," Grundil announced.

Angie stared at them a moment, shocked. "You thought I was some deadly assassin?"

"Vell, some of us did," Grundil said, frowning at George. "But now, based on vhat Béla told us, ve see you have a serious problem. Ve think ve can give you some information that might help you; but after that, you must continue vith this on your own. It is too dangerous, and ve have decided ve aren't interested in it any longer."

"I see," Angie said, although she really didn't. But to get some information, she'd agree to almost anything at this point.

They told her that they'd been watching a man called Colonel Ortega, a man with delusions of grandeur, striving to be big, powerful, and profitably corrupt. Actually, he was already corrupt—it was the big and powerful part he was still working on. In fact, the only things truly big about him were his ego and his girth.

He was also superstitious and, when crossed, extremely dangerous. They warned her that one could never tell how he'd react to anything, except that it usually wasn't what was expected. Recently, he'd shown interest in the *Valhalla*. His men, and even the colonel himself, had been seen at the harbormaster's office asking about the freighter.

"We thought," George said, "he was waiting for a shipment. The *Valhalla* is a container ship, after all. But that doesn't seem to be the case. I overheard him say the name Hydra. Then one of my old FBI buddies told me he thought the Hydra was on her way to Mazatlán, and that rumor had it she was on a ship. We put two and two together."

"You're right about the Hydra," Angie said. "One of the other passengers is an Interpol agent—I won't say which one—but he's been watching the ship. He told us the Hydra was on it."

"Aha!" Grundil exclaimed. "Livingstone! Now I remember! I knew him many years ago. In Prague. He vas much thinner then, and had long hair. Such a time ve had! Those vere the days." The smug, satisfied smile that flickered across her lips suggested potent memories, much to Angie's amazement—and curiosity.

Well, so much for keeping secrets, Angie thought. "What do you know about the Hydra?"

The four shook their heads. "No one has ever seen her," MacDougall said softly. "That's why everyone is so afraid of her."

"The Hydra's being involved makes sense," Grundil said. "She is a voman who sells trade secrets from von group to another. But vhy vould the colonel vant to meet vith her? He vouldn't have the money to deal vith the Hydra. He may vant to be a big shot vith some international petroleum corporations, but he doesn't have vhat it takes. Like money."

"Petroleum?" Angie said. She looked from one to the other. "Oh, my God. That just might explain it! The Hydra was selling a formula for a new kind of energy. Something that would replace much of the need for oil and gas—cold fusion, supposedly a safe kind of nuclear energy. That was what the colonel wanted from her."

"So if he was working with petroleum corporations," George began, "he probably was going to sell it to them so they could suppress it."

"And," Grundil said, "if that didn't vork, he could always sell to somevon who'd put this cold fusion into production, vhich vould nail, right in the pocketbook, those so-called petroleum friends." She turned to Angie. "Is the formula vhat everyone thinks you have?"

"It's got to be," Angie said. "Livingstone had tried to lay a trap for the Hydra—to capture her as she came looking for it. But he's disappeared. Paavo was looking for him, and now I don't know where Paavo is. I've been wondering if he left any kind of information in our room that might give some hint where he might be. To tell the truth, I'm afraid to go to the room to look for it. Those people—and I don't know if I'm talking about the Hydra or Colonel Ortega—"

"Or both," Grundil said.

"—might still be looking for me." She studied her companions as a thought struck her. "But they aren't looking for the four of you. What if you went up to my room? See if Paavo left any information for me or Livingstone as to where he might be."

The four glanced quickly at one another.

"I don't know. It could be dangerous," Grundil said.

"For me, but not for you," Angie replied. "You aren't involved in any of this."

"Ve aren't, are ve?" Béla asked.

"Just take a peek," Angie begged. "Please. I'm sick with worry about him." These people were her last hope. "Please," she whispered urgently.

"I'll go," George said. "She's right. There's no danger to us."

"I'll go with you," MacDougall said.

"Me too," Béla announced. "And vhen ve find him and this is all over, so you can smile again, I vill cook you my special goulash vith some *palacsinta gundel módra* for dessert."

"Don't tell me," Angie said. "Isn't that a kind of crêpe with . . . a walnut filling and chocolate rum sauce over it?"

"Excellent!" Béla cried. "Vhen I open my

restaurant, you vill be the first von I invite!"

"And Paavo, too," she said, reminding them of their mission.

"Yes." They gave her a sad-eyed gaze, then turned to each other.

"I too vill go vith them," Grundil said. "I must vatch Béla. Ve can't have a restaurant vithout the cook."

"Thank you all so much," Angie said, clasping her hands. "What would I do without you?"

"Remember, we might not find anything there," George warned, dampening her spirits a little.

"I know." She bowed her head a moment, then lifted it again. "But it's better than sitting here doing nothing. I appreciate it more than words can say."

"You vatch," Béla said. "Ve vill be back soon."

33

Unfortunately, Béla was wrong. Angie didn't have to watch very long before she saw the four of them being marched from the building by two men whose right hands were held rigidly and ominously in their pockets. Angie had a good idea why. A black limousine drove up.

"Oh, my God!" Angie covered her mouth to hold back her cries as her four new friends were pushed inside. The limousine quickly pulled into traffic.

She ran from the park, crossed the street, and jumped into a taxi sitting in front of the basilica. "Quick, follow that limo!" she shouted.

"Is this a movie, *señorita?*" the cab driver asked.

"No. Hurry!"

He tore away from his parking space and sped down the street. "Not too close!" she cried. "Those people might be dangerous. *Peligro!*"

The driver slowed down.

Angie kept turning around to see if Livingstone or Paavo was following as well. But she seemed to be alone in the chase.

The cab headed south and soon left the town far behind. The driver must have seen plenty of movies where one car follows another, because he knew enough to keep back quite far, so far that at times Angie feared they'd lost the limousine. But then the road would straighten ever so slightly, and she'd see it up ahead.

Suddenly her driver pulled off the road and stopped. "What are you doing?" she screamed. "We're going to lose them."

"I am sorry," he said. "I can go no farther, *señorita*."

"Why not?" She stared anxiously ahead as if through sheer willpower she could keep the other car in view.

"The land beyond here . . . we are already too close. It is not safe."

"Why?"

"It is owned by a man called Colonel Ortega. He is a very powerful man. I do not advise following any car going to visit his hacienda."

Ortega! She'd learned about him from her fearsome four friends, and wondered what the cab driver knew. "Is he a good man or a dangerous one?" she asked.

"I would never say anything bad about the colonel," the driver said. "But I would not want to be found on his property unless I was invited. . . . And I would not want to be invited."

"Oh, dear."

"We should go back before someone sees us. I hope it is not already too late."

"Not too late . . . for many people," she murmured.

An hour later, Angie was once again in the plaza across from the Hotel del Sud. Once again she called the front desk and asked to speak with Paavo or Dudley Livingstone, and once again she was told that neither man answered his phone.

She sat on the same park bench she had sat on previously, when Béla and the others spoke with her. But now she felt more alone than ever. There was no one left to help her. Nowhere to turn.

Why had the colonel's men kidnapped her friends? She shut her eyes against the possibilities. It didn't make sense. None at all. Tears spilled from her eyes, but she blinked them angrily away.

She could go to the police. But would they listen? It was clear that the colonel was a man of some influence. What if he controlled some of the local gendarmes? And what if she picked the wrong gendarme to go to with her troubles?

She could end up making things a lot worse. But she had to do something. And soon.

Maybe she should call Yosh? But it would take him a day to get here—if his passport was in order. That might be too late.

She covered her face with her hands. Paavo had told her to go back to the States. He'd warned her. He was probably right. It was the only prudent thing to do. And she was always prudent . . . sort of. But how could she leave?

She gazed across the plaza at the basilica of Mazatlán and prayed for all she was worth.

Suddenly a voice cried out, "Hey!"

Startled, she almost looked upward. Then reason prevailed. She knew that voice. Standing up, she searched the faces of the people behind her.

"Hey! Miss Amala . . . Angie. Hold it!"

She turned to see Ruby Cockburn hurrying her way. The bun on the top of her head was askew, and the wispy strands around her face flew about more wildly than ever. Angie had never seen an old person move that fast.

"What's wrong?" she asked.

"Trouble all around." Gasping for breath, she held on to Angie's arm as she gave a harsh, beady-eyed stare, first to one side, then the other. "Got to talk. Where can we hide out?"

"How about right here?" Angie suggested. "I've got to keep an eye on the hotel. I've been gone too long already, and Paavo might return."

"Return from where?"

"That's the problem. I don't know where he is," Angie cried, glad to have somebody to talk to, even if it was the not-so-sympathetic Ruby.

Her grip tightened on Angie's arm. "It's bigger than I thought!" As soon as they sat, Ruby launched into her story. "Last night, about twenty hundred hours, four men stole on board. Asked about some Hydra. A woman, from what I gather."

Angie stared at her in shock. "They came on the *Valhalla*?" She wondered if they were the same men she had seen leading her spy friends to the limousine.

"One of them grabbed me. Nervy sucker." Ruby frowned.

"Did he hurt you?"

"Hurt me? Felt me up! Would have been more of a thrill if I hadn't been so damned pissed off. Actually, wasn't half bad, till he worked up to my topknot and tried to pull it off my head. Said it had to be a fake. Wonder what he meant by that? Anyway, I kneed him."

Angie's eyebrows rose.

"Never fails to make a man curl up and scrub the mission. Then I beat him with the shuffle-board stick, ran like the dickens, and hid."

"Thank goodness," Angie cried. "What about the Neblers? Was Nellie hurt?"

"Weren't there. Missed the whole thing." Ruby looked disgusted. "Marv wanted to take in some shows. Girlie shows. Nellie went with him. Said he might get himself in trouble if she didn't. Don't know why she thought that. At his age, if he could get into trouble, it'd be a damned miracle."

"At least she was safely off the ship." Angie sighed with relief. "And Harold's okay?"

"Last I saw him, he was asleep. Hearing aid was off and he was out. He could sleep through World War Three."

"So, did those men find the woman they were looking for—the Hydra?"

"Don't know. At one point—they were getting kind of rough—said the Hydra always hung around with a big, good-looking guy. Told them the only men on board worth giving a second nod to was your man and the cook, Mike Jones."

"So, did they look for Mike? Did they find him?"

"Don't know. Like I said, I was out of there. Made me feel bad even saying that much." Then she gave Angie a knowing eye. "For a time."

"What do you mean?"

"Like I said, I went and hid. No foxholes around, but one of those containers on the main deck had a lock missing, and I jumped in and pulled it shut. Nearly scared the life out of me when I did, though. Julio was inside."

Angie's head was spinning. "Julio?"

"Told me he was hiding from Mike Jones, of all things! He swore Jones had tried to kill him. Made me glad I ratted on him, the ingrate! Julio's a good steward."

Mike Jones! Angie felt her skin go cold. "Jones tried to kill Julio? But why?"

"That's what we came to your friend to find out. He's the detective. Let him detect. After everyone left the ship, I checked on Harold—he was still sleeping—got some necessities, and me and Julio came to find you." She looked around, then waved at a man wearing dark glasses and a backward baseball cap. "I told him he needed a disguise. That one seems to work for guys in movies these days. Don't know why, though. Never saw the Duke in any sissy baseball cap, backward or forward."

"*Señorita!*" Julio ran up to her. "We were walking all around searching for you, and here you are." He pressed a hand against his heart. "I was so scared that you had been killed by that crazy man. Now he wants to kill me! And I haven't even done anything!"

She was amazed that they had found her. Talk about a sight for sore eyes. "I'm glad to see you. Both of you."

"Your friend must help us!" Julio wailed. "Did Mrs. Cockburn tell you all about the terrible things that are happening? That Mike Jones tried to kill me?"

"It's so horrible!" Angie cried. It made sense, though, when she remembered Jones's peculiar reaction to her tote bag. If he'd been the mysterious intruder in her room and he wanted to search the bag she carried with her all the time, what better way to get his hands on it than to have her bring it to the kitchen? "But he must be the one behind all this! Not some mythological Hydra at all, but Mike Jones. A man."

"We can take him," Ruby declared.

Angie's spine stiffened. They could stop him. They *would* stop him. "I knew there was something strange about that Mike Jones," she said, furious at how he'd fooled them.

"Yes. It is very strange." Julio paled as the impact of what he'd been through hit him again. "I know your friend is a cop. I hope he can protect me and stop Jones. Maybe talk to the police. I am afraid to go to them. I do not think they will listen to some steward from Chile, anyway. But if Inspector Smith goes to them—"

"Inspector Smith is missing."

Julio's eyes widened.

Angie looked from Julio to Ruby and motioned for them to bend closer to her. "I believe a man called Colonel Ortega either has him or knows where he is," she said quietly. "And maybe Dudley Livingstone, too. He also has four other friends of mine. We've got to get them away from him."

"I have heard of Colonel Ortega." Julio's voice quivered. "He is very powerful. If he has four or five or six of your friends, I think I do not want to be your friend. I am sorry, *señorita*." He stood. "I will try to find someone else to help me."

She and Ruby jumped up and grabbed him, pushing him back down on the bench.

"Where's your fighting spirit, boy?" Ruby demanded.

"It fought and lost," Julio cried.

"Deserter," Ruby snorted.

"You can't leave," Angie said fiercely, standing over him. "Who else but Paavo can protect you from Jones and whoever else he's working with?

You're in danger because of this, too, for some reason. There's a whole criminal conspiracy after you!"

He tried to stand, but she pushed him back down again. He protested. "What conspiracy? How can I be part of something if I do not understand what it is?"

"Stiffen your backbone, boy!" Ruby yelled, jumping to her feet and socking the air. "And fight, fight, fight!"

She was starting to draw a crowd. Angie sat down again. "We need each other, Julio. Without us, they'll all be after you. You won't stand a chance."

"After me for what?" he cried, his arms wide, his eyes desperate.

Angie leaned close. "That's the secret."

He slumped. Ruby didn't say anything; she was too busy pumping the air. Angie grabbed her arm and pulled her down on the bench.

"I do not understand what is this Hydra," Julio said, sounding completely depressed now. "Is it after me, too?"

"I don't think the Hydra exists," Angie said. "I think the one behind all that's happened is Mike Jones. That would make sense. That's why no one has ever seen this Hydra—why she's supposed to be almost magical. It's because she's not real. She's a figment of Mike Jones's imagination. A made-up person. A sort of Remington Steele."

"*Señorita*, I am more confused than ever."

"She's on to something," Ruby said to Julio, then looked down her long nose at Angie. "Even if she is a bit pushy."

Quickly, Angie told them both about Livingstone's explanation of the situation. "Someone has screwed up royally, and we're taking the fall for it. Be a man, Julio! Help me."

"I would, but . . . but I am too tired. Last night I could not even sleep. I stood in the container all night."

"Pull yourself up by your bootstraps, boy," Ruby chimed in. "Remember the halls of Montezuma. Fifty-four forty. Win one for the Gipper!"

"What's a gipper?" he cried.

"It's before my time, too," Angie said.

Ruby looked at the sky and shook her head. "I've got what you two need," she said. She handed Angie the lime green plastic bag she carried. "Those were the necessities I went back for. Don't open it—just peek."

Angie did. Inside the bag were two guns, one large and one small. "What—"

"Always come prepared. Especially when traveling to some godforsaken place with foreigners. Around the U.S., too."

"But . . . how old are they?" Angie had heard some old guns could blow up in your hand.

"Couple months. Got them for me and Harold for this trip, along with a couple others I still have on me. In the bag, one's a ninemillimeter, other's a snub-nosed thirty-eight.

Serious stuff—real firepower. Shells and cartridges included." She looked from Angie to Julio. "You two do know how to use them?"

"I think so," Angie said.

Julio swallowed and nodded.

"Good." Ruby stood. "Some things are better left with youngsters. I'm going to find a hotel for me and Harold till this blows over." She got up to leave. "*Adiós,* and good luck, you two."

"Thanks," Angie murmured as she watched her go.

Her gaze met Julio's.

"I do not know what to do now," he said, almost in tears.

"I do." Then, with a lot more conviction in her voice than she had in her heart, she announced, "Because I've got a plan."

He gazed at her. "A plan, *señorita?*"

"That's right. But first we need to make a few purchases."

34

"Do you know what he is?" the colonel shouted at the Hydra, who was seated on an easy chair in his living room. Ortega couldn't sit. He was too busy stomping back and forth in front of the plate-glass window that looked out over his hillside. "He is an American cop! What the hell were you thinking of?"

She gritted her teeth. She hated working with the insane—an occupational hazard in this business—and the colonel was definitely among the crazies. "He's got the microfilm."

"The hell he does! I was going to have my men beat it out of him when we went through his pockets and found the identification. Now what? How do I let him go? But if I kill him and his death is traced back here, all I have worked for will be over. Ruined!"

"No one will trace it back."

"No? Half of Mazatlán is here already! You,

your toy boy, the cop, that strange group of four foreigners. *Madre mia!* Why did I ever get mixed up with you in the first place?"

"Greed, Colonel Ortega." She crossed her legs, allowing the slit in her tight black skirt to reveal plenty of leg, then struck a match and lit one of the Cuban cigars the colonel kept in his high-priced humidor. She loved a good Cuban. And she didn't necessarily mean a cigar. "It's the same reason everyone gets mixed up with me." She blew the smoke in his direction.

He glared but chose to ignore the insult for the moment. "Then I regret the day I met you." He spat out the words as if they were bullets.

"You aren't the first man who's said that." She breathed in the smoke and held it before letting it roll from her mouth. "Nonetheless, the damage is done. Since Amalfi and Smith don't have the microfilm, and we shredded everything in their room trying to find it, it's got to be on the woman. It had to have been hidden in or on something that she carries or wears all the time—except those few moments when Ingerson was hiding it. We have to get our hands on her."

The colonel stood in front of her, so angry that a vein pulsed on his forehead. "You mean, with all the people I already have imprisoned here, I need another one?"

"Colonel, don't give yourself a stroke." She stood and took a long time snuffing out the cigar in the ashtray before she gazed up at him. "I'll get her for you."

"For *me*? Now I am supposed to kidnap some American woman?" He flung his arms over his head in frustration and anger. "Is it not enough I already have an American cop here? Do you want to bring the whole FBI and CIA down on my neck?"

"All right!" She didn't like to raise her voice, but with some people, it couldn't be helped. "I'll take care of getting rid of them for you, but the price has just gone up another million. Two million dollars now."

Ortega's face turned dangerously livid. "Why should I pay you two million for something you already screwed up?"

"Because you need me to clear it up for you," she said with a smile.

"I would recommend that you go along with her, my colonel," Eduardo Catalán said from where he was docilely sitting. "At this point, there is not a lot of choice."

"Listen to your *consigliore*, Colonel." The Hydra gave Eduardo a slight bow. "He's giving good advice."

Ortega, too, glanced at Eduardo. After a long pause, he sighed. "I suppose the money could come from the same place as the first million."

"But of course, my colonel." Clearly, Eduardo understood perfectly what Ortega had just proposed. "It goes without saying."

Ortega faced her. "All right. We have a deal. Get the woman and find that microfilm. If you cannot, you are dead."

She nodded. "Now, if you'll release my friend Michael, we'll get started."

"It is so hot, *señorita*," Julio said as he crawled out from among the trees and shrubs of the hillside to the road above. "Do you not think we could drive a little closer to the hacienda?"

"We can't chance it," Angie said, following behind him. "And the higher we go, the less vegetation there will be to hide the jeep."

"But it is too hot," Julio cried as they began the long trudge up the road to the colonel's land.

"You aren't half as hot as I am, believe me," Angie said. "We took a chance driving this far."

"But *señorita*—"

"Julio, stuff it."

An hour later they reached the gate to the Ortega compound. Angie could scarcely breathe from the heat.

"Are you sure?" Julio asked. He was so scared, the hand he'd placed on the bell rope shook.

"I'm sure," she said. "Remember, you've got to do the talking. Your Chilean accent is one thing, but if they hear my American accent, it's all over."

He crossed himself. "Perhaps, *señorita*, we need to think of a new plan."

"Oh, for crying out loud," Angie said. She grabbed hold of the bell rope and pulled hard several times, then stepped back and bowed her head.

"*Hijo de puta!* Who the hell do you think you are, ringing that goddamn bell so loud?" A voice yelled from somewhere inside. "I am not deaf!" Angie understood a little Spanish, but she didn't need a translation to get the full flavor of the guard's words. He pulled open the wooden gate. Scowling and red-faced, he peered out at them.

"Oh!" The man's eyes widened as he looked from Angie to Julio. "Excuse me, Father," he said to Julio, bobbing his head respectfully, then turned to Angie. "Sister, pardon me, please. I meant no disrespect," he murmured with a deep bow of his head.

"I am sorry to disturb you, my son," Julio said, also speaking in Spanish, as he carefully followed Angie's prior instructions. He pressed the pads of his fingers together, bowing his head slightly and talking in the meek yet self-assured tone of the very pious. "Sister Dominique is feeling faint. I wonder if we could trouble you for some cold water? Our canteens are nearly dry." His voice grew stronger as he became more comfortable with his new role.

"What are you doing up here, Father?" the man asked, still incredulous at the sight before him.

"We are going up there to bless this mountain." Julio pointed toward the top of the mountain, its craggy summit high above the gate.

"No one goes up there," the guard said. "There is no road. The road ends here. This is private land."

"We have no choice," Julio said wearily.

"Why is that?" The man scowled, for the first time showing some hostility.

This isn't going to work, Angie thought.

But she hadn't anticipated Julio's capacity to slip into the role of a priest. He inched closer to the guard, his voice low. "Have you ever felt the presence of evil spirits on this hill?" He didn't wait for an answer. "Be careful!" he warned with a shout. "Sister Dominique is from France, from Lourdes, where she has seen many miracles. And where, also, she has been prevented from learning Spanish, I am sorry to say."

The guard studied Angie with renewed interest.

"Three days ago, as we prayed in our little church in Topolobampo, Sister felt something evil fly over our church. It seemed to be strangling her. We left the church to find it, to stamp it out. For three days and nights we have walked or ridden on farmers' carts, without more than a few hours of sleep. We kept moving, driven by Sister Dominique's vision. That is why we are so very, very tired." Angie noticed that he said those last words with true feeling. "But she would not, could not stop."

As the guard scrutinized Angie, Julio took a deep breath, then continued his explanation. "The evil led us to this mountain. Yesterday it was particularly strong—yesterday the evil was everywhere. I hope it did not trouble you."

"Here?" The man looked puzzled, yet a line

of worry had begun to crease his brow.

Angie handed Julio a small vial. "We have brought some holy water," Julio said. "From Lourdes. Perhaps this house as well as the hill needs to be sanctified."

Angie stepped up to the man. The top of her head barely reached his shoulder. She lifted her hand to his head and with her thumb made a cross on his forehead. Thank God she'd had the foresight to remove her nail polish, or they couldn't have gotten past the gate. The guard's eyes met hers. She could see he was mustering the courage to turn the two of them away, as she knew any guard worth his salt should do.

One last chance. She stared at him, opening her eyes wide, then shut them and fell to the ground.

"She has fainted! *Dios!* Help us!" Julio appeared to grow more hysterical by the second. "Something here must have frightened her. Sister! Wake up!" He knelt down and patted her face, but she kept her eyes shut.

"My son," Julio implored the guard, "will you not help us? Some water? Some bread? Perhaps a moment or two out of this infernal heat." He stood and lifted Angie in his arms, teetering slightly. "Is there anyplace I can care for her until we are ready to travel once more? Perhaps if I speak with the owner of this hacienda, tell him about this nun . . . this saint, tell him we are here . . ."

"What is all the commotion?" Another guard

came running to them. "I saw that you had the gate open, Manuel. What is the problem?"

"These two," Manuel said. "The nun fainted and the priest looks ready to pass out as well."

"A nun fainted at the gate? That is all the colonel needs to hear." The second guard crossed himself. "*Madre mia!* Come, Father. Follow me." As Manuel locked the gate again, the second guard led them up to the main house. "Can I help you carry her?"

"No," Julio replied. "To me, her weight is no more than a feather."

"She is very pretty, is she not?" the guard said stepping a little closer.

"Her soul is beautiful," Julio replied. A very noble answer—Angie had to give him credit.

"You are both young and handsome," the guard continued. "It must be hard to treat each other like a nun and a priest all the time, hey?"

She felt Julio shift uneasily. "But we are a nun and a priest all the time." His voice grew a bit choked. "She is a sister to me, and my heart is with God."

"You are still a man," the guard said knowingly.

Julio sighed. "Sometimes I have to pray very hard," he admitted woefully.

The guard laughed, and the sound of his footsteps seemed to grow a bit lighter.

35

Angie felt herself being placed on top of a bed. Then a cool, small hand touched her forehead. She opened her eyes.

"Sister, forgive me if I woke you. We were worried about you." The woman leaning over her was in her fifties, with a round face, black eyes, and long, graying hair pulled back and braided Indian-style. Her dress was a colorful cotton print.

"I am Sylvia, Colonel Ortega's housekeeper." She handed Angie a cup of cold well water. It was so pure and refreshing, Angie couldn't help but wonder why water didn't taste this good back home. She'd been warned about not drinking unboiled water in Mexico, but she hoped that in this case she could get away with it.

"Thank God you are awake, Sister Dominique," Julio said from the other side of the bed. "Are you feeling better?"

Angie nodded. Julio hastened to explain to the guard and Sylvia, "The good sister can understand a little Spanish, but she is far too shy and otherworldly to attempt to converse in it." He turned again to Angie.

"These fine people are letting us stay for a few hours until you are once again on your feet. I will be in the kitchen." Then he stepped back. "My daughter"—he addressed Sylvia as if she were a young girl, despite the fact that she was obviously a good thirty years his senior—"let us allow the sister to rest."

"I will fix her something to eat to restore her strength," Sylvia said. "My husband, Raúl"—she gestured at the guard who had led them to the house—"has told me that the sister is a saint, brought here to save us from evil." Sylvia's eyes shone with faith.

"Sister Dominique is very special," Julio said. "She will eat later. First, she must sleep. Let us leave her alone for now."

"Of course." Sylvia squeezed Angie's hand and left.

As soon as their footsteps died away, Angie jumped up from the bed. She waited a moment, then stuck her head into the hallway. It was empty. She darted down it.

If anyone noticed her, she could say—in a soft-spoken, embarrassed mixture of her fluent French and limited Spanish, which would, she hoped, hide her American accent—that she was looking for the bathroom.

The hacienda appeared to be only one story, in the way of many Spanish-style homes in Mexico. After a quick search, she couldn't find anywhere that prisoners might be held on the main floor. At the back of the house, though, she found a staircase that led down to a basement, possibly to what had been built as a wine cellar or a place to store food.

She had started to tiptoe down the stairs when, partway down, she heard men's voices. She almost fainted with relief. Paavo and her new friends, surely! Listening hard, she concluded that their words didn't have the intonations of Spanish, though she wasn't sure they were speaking English, either. Still, it had to be them. And if so, very likely a guard was with them.

Somehow, she was going to have to get down into the cellar to find out for sure if the voices belonged to Paavo and the others. If she was wrong, she'd have to continue her search elsewhere. She couldn't base her actions on assumptions.

She needed to come up with something clever. But what? Easing herself back up the stairs to the hallway, she was trying to figure out what to do next when she heard footsteps approaching. She flung herself to her knees in front of a window, bowing her head against the sill as if in prayer.

"Sister!" Julio cried. "Here you are."

She glanced at him and shook her head,

wanting him to leave her alone to go on with her investigation.

"What is wrong?" The guard, Raúl, stepped up to her from behind Julio.

Damn! Angie thought, her eyes begging Julio to get rid of the guard.

"Something is wrong with the house," Julio said. "We must sanctify it. Pray over it. I think you should leave us here alone so we can concentrate."

"But I told you," Raúl protested, "I have orders to bring you both to the colonel. He is asking for you. Colonel Ortega is a very important man. And a religious man. He wants to meet you both."

There wasn't anything they could do but agree.

"As you wish," Julio said. "Come, Sister." He helped Angie to her feet and she walked heavily forward, leaning on him as if still very ill.

The two were led into a massive game room where Ortega was playing billiards. He put down the cue as they entered.

"Ah! You do me great honor," he said, walking to their side. He shook Julio's hand and beamed when Angie clasped his hand in both of hers. "I understand you are on a pilgrimage of some kind."

"Yes, to bless this mountain," Julio said.

"Does she not speak?" the colonel whispered to Julio.

"She speaks very little. She is from France, so her Spanish is poor."

Ortega nodded, studying Angie. He turned to Julio once more. "Why do you want to bless the mountain?"

"Three days ago, Sister had a vision. It led us to this place."

"A vision? Of what?" Ortega asked. "Not that I believe in such things, Father."

"I am afraid Sister Dominique's words did not make any sense to me," Julio said. "She talked about an evil one. A man or woman who carried a magic elixir that would do great harm. Many people on this hill will die because of that elixir."

"She said that?" Ortega put his cigar down, his eyes widening.

"Yes. It is crazy talk, but she was so certain, she alarmed me. So we came. Forgive us for bothering you. We will leave as soon as she is strong enough to walk."

"Wait," the colonel demanded. "Do not be so hasty."

"But we have seen your home here," Julio said. "It is very nice. Very beautiful. I am sure there is nothing evil here. I must not have understood Sister Dominique correctly."

"*No!*" Angie shouted, causing both Ortega and Julio to jump.

"I am sorry, Colonel Ortega," Julio said quickly. "Sometimes she gets very emotional. She is a saint. What can I say? We will leave you. I am sorry we bothered you."

Ortega clutched Julio's arm. "Stop, please," he implored. "If Sister Dominique says she must drive out devils, I will not dispute that. My mountain is your mountain. You must spend the night here."

"You are too kind," Julio said. "But we should, perhaps, leave tonight."

"It will be dark before you get very far," the colonel warned.

"We will join you for dinner, then," Julio said. "But afterward, we will be leaving."

"I demand that you stay!" Ortega insisted, growing a little testy. Almost immediately he seemed to realize that it might not be smart to demand anything of these two, and so he smiled and opened his arms wide. "Please, Father, Sister. This evil she speaks of worries me. Bless my house. It is all I ask."

Angie gestured for Julio to bow his head close to hers so that she could whisper to him.

As Ortega watched them, the line of his jaw grew increasingly belligerent. "What does she say?"

"Nothing," Julio said, clearly lying. "I believe we need to leave right after dinner. She will be all right."

"Leave? Why? What is wrong?"

"Nothing. She is confused." Julio took Angie's arm and turned toward the door. "Nothing at all."

"Tell me!" Ortega drew his gun. Julio paled, and Angie grabbed his arm, the two of them staring wide-eyed at the colonel.

"She—" Julio cleared his throat. "She said

that all of you are dead men. That forces of darkness surround you."

Angie crossed herself and then, thankful she'd learned some prayers in Latin years ago, clasped her hands, bowed her head, and began to drone softly. *"Sancta Maria, mater Dei . . ."*

"Why is she doing that? Stop her!" Colonel Ortega yelled. "There is no problem here."

"Ora pro nobis peccatoribus nunc . . ."

"She feels it is not safe," Julio said. "Something is amiss here. You must do what you can to change your destiny. Man has free will. He should use it to be safe, to do good deeds, to not harm innocents."

"Et in hora mortis nostrae . . ."

Colonel Ortega's face reddened as he looked from one to the other and the meaning of the prayer became clear. "Get out of my sight! But do not leave this house!"

"Amen."

Julio and Angie hurried from the room and down the hall to the kitchen. "I heard voices in the basement," she whispered to him. "It sounded as if they were speaking English, but I'm not sure."

"That must be where they were put," Julio said. "I have looked all around the main floor and out in the garden. I do not see anyplace else where they could hide so many people. This is too dangerous for us to handle. If you heard them, they are still alive. We need to get the police—somehow convince them to help us."

"Sure. They'll come here and ask the colonel if he's holding any foreigners prisoner. You think he'll confess? Be reasonable."

"But we cannot stay," Julio whined. "You heard Ortega. He is crazy."

"But he's also, in his primitive way, a believer, and we've rattled him. Time for Plan B."

"Ah! Plan B. Good," he cried. "I hope it works better than Plan A."

"Thanks for your confidence."

Julio went off to look around the hacienda while Angie hurried toward the kitchen. She heard someone walking around in it.

Holding her hand to her heart and curving her shoulders as if she had a lung condition, she stumbled through the door.

"Sister!" cried Sylvia, who was bent over the stove, stirring something in a kettle. "You should be lying down. You do not look well."

"I must help," Angie said in her broken French-Spanish. She glanced over the kitchen quickly, then at the pot of beans Sylvia was cooking. She stirred them a moment, then tasted one. They would do, perfectly.

Then Angie turned back to Sylvia, patting her on the shoulder and then motioning for her to sit down at the table. She did, looking confused. Angie poured a cup of coffee from the coffeemaker on the counter and carried it to Sylvia, then looked around the kitchen until she found some crispy, sweet *buñuelos*. She took two to

Sylvia, then sat beside her with a smile.

"Oh, Sister, you are so kind," Sylvia said, stunned. Then, to Angie's surprise, the woman's eyes grew misty. "I work hard here and get so tired, and nobody appreciates . . . or notices . . ."

Taken aback, Angie squeezed the woman's hands and smiled at her. Then she went to the cupboards, pulling out spices she'd need.

"But . . . but . . ." Sylvia stood up. Angie understood the look on her face, the offended look of a cook who's just had someone take over her kitchen uninvited.

"*Está bien,*" Angie said as she began to season the beans to make a pot of chili. She knew it was basically an American southwestern food that had found its way over the border to Mexico's northern states. But perhaps this far south, it'd seem special.

As Angie cooked, Julio came into the kitchen. Seeing the tortured expression on Sylvia's face, he began to work his considerable charm on the woman, keeping her out of Angie's way. Angie brought him a cup of coffee and *buñuelos,* as she had Sylvia. His gaze warmed upon her, for just a moment, in a most unpriestly way.

After nearly a quarter hour of inconsequential chatter with Sylvia, he said, "My daughter, I fear there is much evil here. You see how weak Sister Dominique is growing? It is killing her. She is trying to fight it, but she cannot."

"Is the evil Colonel Ortega?" Sylvia asked, her eyes wide and fearful.

"I do not understand who or what it is. Sister says it is someone else. But we do not see any men or women who do not belong here. She must be mistaken."

As Sylvia hung on Julio's every word, Angie took a small bottle of chloral hydrate from the deep pocket of her habit and poured it into the pot of beans—otherwise known as slipping a mickey to whoever ate them. The drug had been a very simple black-market purchase. Julio had done himself proud that afternoon, she thought. As she'd hoped of a seaman who'd been to many cities throughout the world, he hadn't taken long to connect with the sort of people who could find him whatever he wanted for a price. And Angie had readily come through with whatever price they had required.

To the beans, she added lots more ground chilies, cumin, and cilantro to help mask the taste of the drug, if any.

"I know who this evil one is you are speaking about, Father," Sylvia said, moving closer to Julio. "A strange woman was here. But this morning she left. I did not like her from the moment she stepped into this house, flaunting all her airs!"

"You mean Sister may have been feeling the evil presence of some woman, not just a spirit?" Julio asked. He made eye contact with Angie.

"Yes. A real woman. Alive—but perhaps not much longer. She was supposed to give something to the colonel, but she has not done it yet.

He is furious with her. Tonight, if she does not
show up with it, he might have her . . . well, I
should not say. But he is not a good man either,
I am sorry to tell you."

Julio looked ready to faint. Angie dropped
the spoon she'd been using to stir the chili, and
as it fell to the floor with a loud clatter, it jarred
Julio into looking at her. She stared hard at him,
willing him to pull himself back together.

He faced Sylvia again. "I . . . I see," he said,
his voice a nervous squawk. He crossed himself,
clasped his hands together, and whispered some
prayers of a sort Angie had never heard before.
She was impressed. He was really getting into
this.

Sylvia waited. Finally Julio stopped praying.
"Sister Dominique and I will leave tonight, after
dinner. You have given me much encouragement that we have not wasted our time here."

"Father, please, do not abandon us!" Sylvia
grabbed Julio's hands tight.

Angie walked up to her, turned her from
Julio, and gently laid her hands on both of
Sylvia's cheeks. Julio rushed to interpret. "She
means that it will be all right," he said to Sylvia.
"Rest now. She will serve the dinner tonight."

"Thank you." Sylvia pulled a handkerchief
from her pocket and dabbed at her eyes as she
left her kitchen.

"So, the Hydra really is a woman," Angie said,
grabbing Julio's arms. "And she's been here."

"Yes," Julio replied in an accusing voice, "and

if she had been here when we came and she was someone from the freighter, she would have recognized us! Then what? We would have been killed."

"What could we do? We had to take the chance. If she'd been here and seen us, we would have gone to Plan C."

"What was that?"

"Run."

Julio's expression turned more glum than ever. "I think that should have been Plan A."

36

The door to the basement cell swung open, startling the prisoners. George Gresham was booted into the small room, where he collapsed on the cement floor. The door slammed shut behind him.

"George, are you all right?" Grundil knelt at his side and turned him onto his back. "Vas he torturing you very horribly?"

Béla let out a muffled, terror-stricken cry.

Shawn MacDougall, who had been sitting on the floor in a far corner of the cell, scooted back further against the wall and wrapped his arms tightly around his legs.

George groaned and slowly drew himself into a sitting position. His face had a red, swollen mark on one cheek. "I'm all right. They only hit me a couple of times. More than anything, I need water."

"What did they want from you?" Paavo asked, standing over him.

George ran his hand over his crew cut. "The colonel wanted to know what I knew about the formula—apparently it's on microfilm. Heck, I didn't even know that much about it. I was asked why the Hydra won't give it to the colonel. And why I was so stupid as to go into your room looking for you. That was the only question I could answer. I agreed with him—I was stupid!"

The door opened once more, and the black eyes of the guard searched the prisoners a moment before they stopped on Paavo. "You. Come."

Paavo followed him out the door and up the stairs to a gaudy living room with a wall of glass that looked out over the lush green jungle at the foot of the mountain. It looked out, Paavo thought, over freedom.

Colonel Ortega sat in a high-backed leather wing chair, smoking a cigar.

"Sit down," the colonel said, politely gesturing to Paavo to sit in another leather chair across from his own. "You are—?"

"John Doe," Paavo said.

The colonel shook his head, his expression bored and unsympathetic. "Yet another John Doe. There are so many of you. It must be a very common name in the U.S."

Paavo didn't reply.

The colonel flicked the ash off the end of his

cigar and blew gently on the tip so that it glowed. "For some reason which I fail to understand, *Inspector Smith,* you and your friends are interfering in my business. And I want to know why."

"Whatever is going on," Paavo replied, "it has nothing to do with me or the others you're holding. In fact, I scarcely know them. We were all staying in the same hotel. That's it."

Colonel Ortega threw his head back and emitted a loud, very fake laugh, then stopped abruptly and stared at Paavo, his gaze hard. "All foreigners tell stupid lies. You are making me angry! I—"

Just then Sylvia came into the room with flowers, incense, candles, and a statue of the Virgin Mary much taller than the one already in one corner of the room. "Excuse me, Colonel Ortega."

"It is all right," Ortega grumbled. "Set it up." He glanced at Paavo. "We had a crazy nun here today. Ignore the servant."

Nun? Paavo's mind raced over the possibilities. *No,* he thought, *couldn't be. She couldn't possibly pull off that one.*

"Why don't you just let us go, Ortega?" he said. "It will bring you nothing but harm to keep us. We can't help you with your problem, whatever it is. Surely, you've realized that by now. We know as little as you do about it."

The colonel leaned forward from his chair and pounded the coffee table. "I want to know where my formula is."

"No one knows," Paavo said. "And besides that, it's not worth a damn thing. Cold fusion doesn't work. It's a scam. Don't you know that?"

The colonel paled. "So you do know about the formula."

"Everybody knows about the formula," Paavo said, easing back into his chair. He had decided that the best hope for all of them was to make sure the colonel questioned everything, no matter how many lies Paavo had to tell to make it happen. The housekeeper placed the statue on a table in front of a mirror and began arranging the flowers around the base of it.

"Everybody knows that your Professor Von Mueller in Berkeley," Paavo continued, "was trying to sell his so-called formula because the government was about to go in and shut him down. The man was a phony. He lied so he could continue to get grant money, continue to lead a good life—"

Ortega jumped to his feet, his face livid. "You are the one who lies!"

"You've seen my passport," Paavo said. "I'm a cop in San Francisco. Berkeley is just across the bay from me. Don't you think I know what's going on right in my own backyard? The only one who's being scammed around here is you— by the Hydra. That's why she won't give you the formula. If she does, you'll find out it's a fake."

"No. No! You are trying to confuse me. Confuse everything."

"If that wasn't the truth, how could I know so

much about it?" Paavo asked, his voice calm and reasonable.

The housekeeper lit the candles and the incense, then hurried out of the room.

"Eduardo?" The colonel turned to the man who had been sitting quietly in a chair in the corner of the room.

Eduardo shrugged in a way that clearly said, *Don't ask me.*

"Damn!" The colonel kicked the coffee table in front of him and stood up, then began pacing and muttering to himself. "Why do I get involved with foreigners? You cannot trust any of them! Not the bad ones, not even the good ones!"

"We'll cause you even more trouble if you don't let us go," Paavo said, his voice and his manner stern and cold. "Tourists disappearing off the streets of Mazatlán? Is that what you want? Investigators will turn the town—maybe even this hilltop—upside down. Lots of people know where we were headed. You think you can stop all of them from talking? From investigating?"

"Perhaps you will all meet with an unfortunate accident," the colonel said. "Your car will go off a hillside into a deep ravine. No survivors. Such a tragedy."

"It doesn't hold," Paavo countered. "We weren't traveling together, and we don't have a car. Look, maybe you caught us trespassing on your property when we were out sightseeing and got lost, okay? That's enough reason to detain us for a short while, but that's all. Let us go."

The colonel spun on him. "Or we can just kill every last lying one of you, and let your friends be damned. I *am* the law on this mountain, Inspector Smith! No one, especially not some *gringo* cop, can tell me what to do."

"You don't even know if the formula works, Colonel Ortega," Paavo said. "Is it really worth destroying everything you've accomplished here? Because that's what will happen if you kill us. Nothing will be the same for you. Think about it."

The strong scent of incense filled the room. Ortega leaned back, breathing it in. "The nun said evil has come to my mountain," Ortega said. "She said it brings death. I fear she is right. The evil is you and your friends!"

"Maybe the evil is your greed," Paavo said quietly.

The colonel's face hardened, and he glanced at the guard. "Take him away."

The guard whacked Paavo hard on the shoulder and motioned for him to stand up. He did, and was kicked and pushed back down to the cellar.

Julio dished rice onto a plate and handed it to Angie. She spooned chili on top of the rice, then sprinkled grated Cotija cheese on top of the chili. The cheese had melted nicely when she took the first plate of food to the colonel

and placed it on the table in front of him. Bowing humbly, she returned to Julio's side and did
the same for Eduardo Catalán.

Catalán watched every move she made—a bit
too closely. He worried her.

The bodyguards who usually ate in the
kitchen had been asked to join the colonel for
this special meal prepared by the hands of a
saintly nun. Quickly, Angie served each of them.

"Sister Dominique would also like to take a
plate of food to the guard at the gate," Julio said
to the colonel, "the guard who was so kind as to
allow us entry, and to any other help you might
have, down to the lowest shepherd."

"There are no shepherds here," said Ortega,
leaving his food untouched as he watched Angie
and Julio. "The guards can wait. You two must
eat first. We would not want to eat this meal and
then find out it, er, was not to the cook's taste,
shall we say? Eat up, Sister, Father."

Angie bowed her head meekly, and she and
Julio sat down. They both began to eat in small
bites, taking as much rice and as little chili as
possible under the watchful eyes of the colonel
and his men.

"It is delicious, Sister, as always," Julio said. He
reached for the shredded Cotija and added a bit
more on top, then pushed it onto the warm
chili, watching it melt. Angie, too, added more
Cotija, trying not to make it too obvious that
they were playing with their food more than eating it. The others sat and watched.

Finally, Angie took a big mouthful of food, mostly rice, and let some of the juice from the chili dribble from the side of her mouth. She used her forefinger to scoop it up, then put her finger against her mouth, making a slight sucking sound as she pulled it away—finger-lickin' good being the message she hoped to convey. Julio smiled and nodded, as if he too was greatly enjoying the meal. Much as she did, he took a large forkful of mostly rice, and gave a little "Mmm" of appreciation as he chewed.

"Pass the cheese," the colonel ordered, impatient with their display while his dinner got cold. Soon everyone was eating heartily.

"It is good," Ortega said. "I have never eaten anything like it."

"It is a northern dish," Julio said as he and Angie stood up. "We must leave you for a moment. Sister Dominique cannot enjoy her meal while she thinks of the men who are hungry at their work stations. We will take food to them, then come back to join you. But first, let us pour you some wine."

From under the table he lifted four bottles of what the housekeeper had told them was the best red wine in the house. They went around the table pouring large glassfuls for each of the men, then went back and refilled the colonel's and Eduardo's glasses.

As soon as that was done, the two of them retreated to the kitchen. "Quick," Angie said. Large mugs of strong coffee sat on the counter.

They had already turned cold, but it didn't matter. They contained the caffeine she and Julio needed to counteract the tiny portion of the drug they'd been forced to eat. In a corner, Sylvia snored loudly. She'd tested the chili as it cooked.

Angie and Julio grabbed bowls and trays and filled them with a little rice and a lot of chili and cheese, took a bottle of wine and glasses, then went in search of the four guards out on the premises. When they found them, the food and wine were eagerly accepted.

But when they returned to the house, to their dismay they heard the colonel and the others still talking in the dining room. They stood in the kitchen, Angie wondering what to do next. Sylvia had passed out within ten minutes after eating some chili. What was wrong? Did the chloral hydrate lose its punch when heated or when exposed to air too long?

Angie was heartsick. Now what?

"We must wait," Julio said. "They are all big men. But . . . but what if it does not work, *señorita?*"

"That's what I've asked myself every minute today," she answered, rubbing her brow in anguish. "If it fails, we go to Plan D."

"I did not know we had a Plan D," he said.

"It's the easiest plan of all—play it by ear."

37

As the time slowly passed and the talk continued, Angie's despair grew. She had to get Paavo away from this place. It was hard to believe that any of this was really happening. From this hilltop, looking down on the lush tropical foliage that surrounded Mazatlán, a part of her wanted to believe this whole episode was a joke of some kind, that she and Paavo faced nothing more dangerous than the set of *Romancing the Stone.*

She wanted to call out "Cut!" and walk away, back to San Francisco and the life she knew and loved. But then she looked down at the nun's habit she had rented at a costume shop, at Julio's black suit and turned Roman collar, and listened to the raucous voices of the men in the dining room.

It wasn't a game. She wanted to cry, to give up and let someone else come up with a plan. But she knew better than to follow that line of thinking. There *was* no one else, and she wasn't about to let Paavo die.

She must be patient.

The waiting was interminable, though. Her eyes grew heavy with lack of sleep and the drug; she drank more coffee and forced herself to stay awake, to watch and listen.

"Julio, we'll have to rush them," she whispered finally. "We've got to do something while we still have a chance at surprise and gaining the upper hand."

"No, *señorita*. They will kill us," he protested. His eyes were begging her not to do anything so scary. "It is too dangerous."

"We have no choice," Angie insisted. She lifted up the skirt of her habit and took out the gun she'd strapped to her inner thigh with the special holster Julio had found for it. She moved it to the pocket of her habit. "Come on, Julio."

"Please, *señorita*." Alarmed, he grabbed her wrist. "There must be a better way."

"There isn't. And I can't stand waiting a moment longer. Let go of me!" She tried to yank her arm away, but his grip tightened. She glared at him. "I'm going to step behind the colonel, then draw the gun and hold it against the back of his head. We tell them all that if they don't free the prisoners, I'll shoot."

"You would not be able to pull the trigger," he said.

"I would." She drew a deep breath. "God help me."

He looked at her a long time, as if he almost believed her. "I still say it is too dangerous for you. And me, too," he insisted.

She shook her head. "I'm sorry." She pushed the door open and walked into the dining room.

"Ah, the little nun has come to join us again," Ortega said. "Sit. Your dinner must be cold as ice by now."

She smiled, then picked up a half-empty wine bottle. *"Más?"* she asked, pulling the cork from the bottle.

The colonel looked at his glass. It was nearly empty. "Of course, I always appreciate more wine. Especially when"—he put his hand in front of his mouth—"when served by one so holy."

"Sister, wait," Julio said, grabbing her arm.

She couldn't believe this. Why was he interfering with her now? It was too late for that.

"Um, before you take the wine away, please pour a little for me, if you would," Julio said.

Has he gone mad? she thought frantically. She wasn't sure what to do—wouldn't the colonel be insulted if she served Julio first?

"On second thought," the colonel said, lifting his hand again to his mouth but this time unable to hide to hide his full-blown, noisy yawn, "I think I will lie down a moment." He eased himself off the chair onto the floor.

Angie's gaze caught Julio's. He must have noticed the colonel yawn earlier while she had missed it.

"Damn," Eduardo said, his voice slurred. His gaze bore into Angie as if he knew what she'd done. But it was too late for him to stop it. "Raúl . . . ," he called, then plopped his head onto the table.

"Yes, Señor Catalán." Raúl stood up. He scratched his belly as he peered sleepily at his bosses. "Hmm, I suppose I am in charge now. But there is something wrong here." He stumbled backward into the wall and opened his mouth in a loud, long yawn. In the middle of the yawn, his legs gave out from under him and he slid down the wall to the floor. His head bobbed forward onto his chest and he was asleep.

All around them the other guards began yawning and curling up on the table or the floor. Angie and Julio stood stock-still, not moving, not doing anything to call attention their way.

Soon a cacophony of snoring was the only sound to be heard.

Angie and Julio tiptoed backward out of the dining room, as unobtrusively as they could, then turned and ran down the hall to the basement stairs. They stood at the top until they were sure they heard the mellifluous sounds of a deep sleep coming from the man who was guarding the prisoners.

As quietly as possible, they tiptoed down the stairs. "Should we tie him up?" Angie asked.

"There is no rope nearby. Let us just go quickly and quietly." Julio slid the key from the guard's belt, then unlocked the cell door.

Paavo and the others stared wide-eyed at Angie in her nun's habit and Julio in a priest's collar. Angie pressed her finger to her mouth, then pointed at the sleeping guard. "Knockout drops," she whispered.

The four ex-spies gave nods and winks of approval. Paavo grabbed her in a crushing hug.

All of them hurried away from the guards. Once out of the house, hidden by the night's darkness, they began to run. Paavo took Angie's hand. It felt so good to feel his strong hand on hers again, she thought her heart would burst.

They were free!

"We've got a jeep hidden in the brush a couple of miles down the road. We were afraid to drive closer," Angie said, picking up her skirts so she could run faster.

"Let's take one of the cars here," George said. He ran into the garage. "I'm damned fast at hot-wiring."

"Good idea," Paavo said.

In no time they had piled into a black Mercedes and were flying back down the hillside to Mazatlán, Paavo at the wheel, Angie and Julio in the front seat with him.

"Wait," Angie said. "Where's Livingstone?"

Paavo glanced at her, and she knew the answer. "I'm sorry," he said.

"But how . . . ?" she cried. "He said it was safe! He said we shouldn't worry!"

"I know." Paavo caught her eye. "It happens. And good men die."

She studied him a moment. "Through no one's fault."

He nodded. "Through no one's fault," he repeated softly.

They were rounding a bend in the road when they saw bright headlights coming straight toward them. Angie held her breath as the approaching car suddenly swung to the side and blocked the road. *Let it be the police here to help us,* she prayed.

But Paavo slammed on the brakes and started to back up the hill.

Out of the car jumped Mike Jones and, with him, a woman. With the Mercedes's headlights directly on her, Angie could clearly make out a short woman with black hair parted on the side, the shorter side combed back, the longer side straight and shiny as it skimmed her forehead, brushing the corner of her eye and falling to about midear. She wore heavy black eye makeup and dark berry-colored lipstick. Her clothes were the green camouflage of a jungle fighter, complete with heavy boots and the X of a bandolier across her breasts. In her hands, she carried an assault rifle.

Jones was dressed similarly, and also heavily armed. But his whole attitude was one of deference to the woman.

At that moment, Angie knew she was looking at the Hydra.

How had she missed her before? Now it was as clear as anything. Without the makeup, with-

out the sexy hairdo—without the assault rifle—
Angie would have seen nobody more threaten-
ing than the plain, quiet, and timid person she
knew as Andrew Brown.

The Hydra and Jones took aim. As the Mercedes backed away, Angie could only stare at
them, knowing that at any second the wind-
shield would shatter in a spray of bullets. Paavo
spun the wheel, threw the car into drive, and
aimed it toward the edge of the road. "Everybody out!" he yelled as the shots began and the
car started to tip over the hill and begin its slide.
Pushing his car door open, he grabbed Angie's
arm and jumped, pulling her with him.

They tumbled into the blackness of the hillside. The crashing and groans around them
told them the others were doing the same. The
car rolled ahead of them down the steep slope,
faster and faster until, with a loud crunch of
metal, it smashed into a tree.

A hail of bullets flew over their heads and ric-
ocheted off the rocks around them.

Paavo shoved Angie behind a tree. She
leaned against it as he stood over her, his palms
pressed to the trunk, both of them panting after
running and tumbling in the dark. "Here,"
Angie cried, shoving a gun in his hands. "Ruby
Cockburn gave it to me. Julio has one, too."

Paavo looked over the 9 mm automatic, then
checked the cartridge. The powerful weapon
was loaded and ready. "Good God," he said.

"We were desperate," she answered.

He peered up to the top of the hill. The Hydra and Mike Jones were slowly advancing toward them, firing as they walked. They thought they were perfectly safe—that killing their prey would be like shooting ducks in a barrel, with the ducks having no means of shooting back. Even so, the Hydra kept behind Mike, using him as her human shield.

"Keep down," Paavo warned Angie. As he started to move away from her, she grabbed his hand.

"Come back safely to me, Inspector," she whispered.

His gaze captured hers, then he nodded and circled away from her, crouching low, heading to the left of their pursuers. He took aim, able to see only their merest outline in the moonlight. "Drop it!" he yelled. When they didn't, he squeezed the trigger.

Mike Jones, hit, cried out.

The Hydra fired and dove for cover. A shot rang out from the other side of the brush. Julio must be shooting—or had had the sense to give up his gun to George or one of the other spies who knew how to use it.

The Hydra returned fire, again and again, as she backed up the hill toward her car.

Angie didn't dare even peek to see what was happening. It was clear from the sounds. The Hydra had too many rounds of ammunition for them to overcome. And now she was going to get away again. *Damn.* Angie thought of Livingstone, how he had given up his life because of that woman, how she'd nearly lost Paavo because of her. But what could they do against her assault rifle?

The Hydra reached her car and backed up to the driver's side, firing as she went. The door had been left wide open. She was easing herself down onto the seat when something pressed against her spine. Immediately, a strong arm snaked around her waist and she was pulled down onto a muscular lap.

"This is rather friendly of you, Hydra," Paavo said, jabbing his gun hard between her shoulders. "Now drop the rifle and put your hands up."

38

On the balcony of a luxurious beachfront villa in an exclusive area of Acapulco, Angie and Paavo sat at a glass table in softly padded chairs. An open bottle of champagne was wedged in an ice bucket at the far side of the table, and glasses of bubbly stood at their elbows. In the center was a platter of shrimp on ice, ringed by a variety of dipping sauces.

"Listen to this," Angie said, holding the *New York Times* open and reading from an inside story. "There's a write-up about the Hydra's attempt to steal the cold fusion formula. It says that her real name is Jane Potter and she's from Kansas City, Missouri. To think, she had everyone believing she was some exotic international assassin. Goes to show you!"

Paavo just shook his head.

"Anyway, it says that the formula was no good. Some chemists from the National Science Insti-

tute went to the Lawrence Lab and studied all
Professor Von Mueller's papers and concluded
his cold fusion formula was a fraud, that it
couldn't even be duplicated." She closed the
paper. "So there was all that trouble for nothing."

"It's tragic," Paavo agreed. "Particularly about
Dudley Livingstone. He was a good man."

Just then, one of the many servants who lived
year-round at the villa stepped onto the balcony
holding a silver tray. A single postcard was on it.

"Correspondencia, señorita," the woman said.

"Gracias," Angie said, feeling like an elegant
lady of leisure as she took the card. How she
loved this villa! She glanced at the back of postcard. "It's from Grundil. She and Béla are in
Costa Rica—and she's going to let him open his
Transylvanian restaurant. What fun!"

"I think they'll like Costa Rica," Paavo said. "I
hear lots of Europeans, as well as Americans, are
moving there these days."

"That's true. Oh, my! She says Shawn Mac-
Dougall found true love with Juanita, and
George Gresham liked being involved in a
shoot-out so much, he took a job as a security
guard at a recycling plant in Boise."

"I doubt he'll find much to shoot at there."

"But just think of all the tins cans he'll have to
practice on." Angie handed the card to Paavo so
he could see it for himself. "So," she said, "the
only one who got away was the colonel."

"Maybe not as far away as you think," Paavo

answered. "When we were locked up in Ortega's cellar, Grundil told me she recognized his right-hand man, Eduardo Catalán, from the days she used to spy in the Middle East and around a number of big oil interests."

"She got around, didn't she?" Angie said, not liking the thought of any woman locked up with Paavo.

"It turns out Catalán was a spy as well, a spy for the oil consortium Ortega had been pretending to work with. They didn't trust Ortega—and as we've learned, they were right not to. He would gladly have sold the formula to someone who wanted to use cold fusion to produce energy, if he could have gotten more money that way. Since the consortium is a group that doesn't like disloyalty, the colonel's sudden disappearance might not have been of his own doing."

"Well, I can't say I'm sorry," Angie admitted, folding the paper and putting it on the table. "But now, after all this news, I think we should talk."

"Isn't that what we've been doing?" He lifted his champagne to take a sip.

"I mean, things have turned out well for our new friends, and I'm glad. Even you—you've realized you do want to stay with the police force, and you will. I think it's time to talk about me and what I want. Things like . . . making commitments. Maybe even—" She paused. "—getting engaged."

He nearly choked. "To be married?"

"What else?"

He put down the champagne. "Isn't that impossible?" he asked in an innocent tone, quite unlike him.

"Whatever are you talking about?" she wondered.

"Nuns can't marry."

She folded her arms. "Inspector Smith, you are such a barrel of laughs. I don't give up that easily, you know."

"So I've discovered."

He slid the newspaper to his side of the table. It was his turn to read it now, but he didn't open it. Instead, he looked across the table at Angie, a simple gesture, yet one that spoke reams about intimacy and companionship. Spending his days . . . mornings . . . nights this way with her was something he could get used to quite easily.

He reached for her hand. "Let me make sure I've got my head back together first. I need to go back to work, back to the life we know."

She caught his eye a moment, then nodded.

He slid his thumb over her fingers. "Is it enough that I commit to thinking about a commitment, Miss Amalfi?"

She smiled. "That sounds just fine—for now, Inspector Smith."

Their joined hands tightened.

Just then there was a long blast from a

foghorn, then another and another.

"The *Valhalla*!" Angie cried, jumping to her feet. "Julio said he'd let us know as they sailed by."

"Bully for him," Paavo said. He still smarted when he thought of the good-bye kiss Julio had given Angie when they disembarked in Acapulco. If it had gone on one second longer, the steward might have found himself greeting guests in a voice an octave higher.

"Let's answer him back," Angie said. "I've got a mirror right in there." On a chair in the living room, just past the balcony door, lay the waist pouch she'd been using. From it she pulled out her compact. She found she'd become rather fond of having her hands free and her shoulders not aching from carting a big purse everywhere with her.

"That won't work," Paavo said. "It's too small."

"I can try. Maybe the Neblers and Cockburns will stop playing bridge long enough to greet us, too. We've certainly given them a lot to talk about for years to come." She walked over to the edge of the balcony, right by the railing, and opened the compact wide. Holding the powder puff against the pressed powder, she twisted and turned it until the mirror caught the sun.

A flash of light from the *Valhalla* sent a return greeting. "Hallelujah! It worked!" she cried, jumping and waving her arms in the air. Suddenly, the compact slipped from her fingers. When it landed, the mirror broke and the tin canister that held the pressed powder bounded out of the plastic case.

"Uh-oh—seven years' bad luck," she said, going to retrieve it.

"In other words, seven years of Julio hanging around," Paavo muttered.

"Wait. What's that?" Angie said, looking among the broken glass.

"Don't cut yourself." Paavo turned to the front page of the newspaper.

"Whatever it is, I guess it can't be the micro-film everyone was looking for. Since it was stuck inside my compact, under the tin of powder, it must be a packaging item of some sort."

"Powder?" Paavo said, his brow furrowed. "Wait, didn't Ingerson say something about powder . . . ?"

She picked up the tiny square and held it up to the sun. "It sure looks like a little piece of film, though."

"You're joking again, right?" Paavo asked, clearly unable to believe this turn of events.

"I'm not! Could it possibly be the film with the formula?" she asked. "Have I been carrying it around all this time?"

"Don't tell me!" Paavo said, starting to get up.

"Well, if it is, I don't want to know!" She flung it over the balcony and watched as the breeze caught it and carried it out over the Pacific.

"Angie!" Paavo shouted, running to the balcony rail. "You didn't. . . ." He scanned the horizon, but the microfilm had disappeared.

"Good riddance is what I say." She brushed off her hands. "For something completely worthless, that poor old professor died, and Dudley died, and Sven Ingerson died, and we could have died. The whole situation was horrible. Just horrible! Besides that, I may never want to take a cruise again as long as I live!" She paused to catch her breath.

"Uh, Angie. . . ," Paavo said quietly.

"What?"

"You know that story in the *Times* about the formula being no good?"

"That's what I'm so mad about! All that death, and then the dumb formula didn't even work!"

"Angie, sometimes the government plants stories like that. It's disinformation. You've got to remember that they didn't know who had the formula. They had no idea where it was or when it might show up again—or with whom. There's a good chance they might have just *said* it was no good, but it really was."

"You mean . . . that might have been a real formula for cold fusion?"

"That's right."

Angie mouth formed into an O. Without another word, she looked from him to the wide expanse of ocean and beach. The microfilm had disappeared out there, lost somewhere between the sand and the sea. Her heart sank as she realized that she might have thrown away the key to solving the energy problems of the twenty-first century.

"Paavo," she said, her voice small. "What do you think about keeping this as our little secret?"